Markus Pfeiler

Her Majesty's Auditor

An Adventure Novel with Steampunk Elements

I0591331

About "Her Majesty's Auditor":

Tasked with auditing the accounts of the Queen's ore mines, auditor Howard Forsyth encounters the notorious and feared administrator of the mines. Soon his life is threatened on an adventurous train ride with steam cars and a steam-powered flying object. This is not how he had imagined Lord Palmerston's audit engagement. Then, when he is suspected of murdering the former accountant, his secret lover, whom no one is supposed to know about, rushes to his aid. Will they both survive? What role does the missing general ledger play? What is the sinister invention for?

Not everyone is what they seem.

About the author:

Markus Pfeiler, born in 1973, loves to bake, cook and write. He enjoys traveling and especially visiting cities and the Caribbean. He is a certified public accountant and lives in Switzerland with his family.

Her Majesty's Auditor
© 2021 Markus Pfeiler

Publisher: Absolute Author Publishing House

Library of Congress Cataloging-in-Publication Data:
Her Majesty's Auditor / Markus Pfeiler
p. cm.

ISBN 978-1-64953-339-5 (Paperback)

Her Majesty's Auditor

An Adventure Novel

with

Steampunk Elements

Markus Pfeiler

markuspfeiler.com

Table of Contents

The train arrived at Victoria, Greene County as a thunderstorm rolled in. The large engines of the locomotive chugged on as the brakes squealed loudly to bring the mammoth vehicle to a slow halt. The dark clouds cast a gloomy shadow on the train station and those who waited to receive the individuals aboard the train. The steam-powered behemoth locked onto the rails, letting out a loud hiss which spewed hot water vapor into the air.

The carriages furthest from the engine opened up first. It had the fewest number of occupants as men accompanied by one or two women walked off the train into horse-drawn carriages that awaited them. The women were dressed in the elegant bell-shaped gowns, with countless pleats sewn in all over with the finest silk money could buy, the dresses being such that their tiny legs were almost invisible under it. Their purses clutched underarm and their other hand clutched in the elbow of the men that accompanied them.

The men in turn were dressed just as extravagantly. Most held gold-tipped canes and suede hats. Their morning coats made from the most premium materials as were the jackets and shirts they wore underneath. They chattered away without a care in the world, with an elegance that could be mistaken for pride. While it was slow and painstaking, the coaches furthest from the engine emptied out and its occupants were safely in their carriages, heading off.

The middle coaches opened up just as the heavens let loose. Howard Forsyth bolted out of the vehicle along with other men alongside him. He hailed a carriage looking to transport travelers for a fare. He spoke quickly, giving the coachman his address. There were only a handful of women in his section of the coach, wives of the men returning from trips with their husbands.

The animal-driven vehicle took off to a slow pace, trying to go around people on foot hurrying to shelter from the rain. As it moved past the train, the final coach opened with people nearly tumbling over one another in a mad rush to get out. It was packed to its maximum with men, most dressed in what many in Greene County would consider as rags. They hauled grimy sacks which contained whatever food they had managed to work for in their time out of town. Some of those bags would serve as items of sustenance for a family of four or five children. Mouths that would greet them first when they could be made from the distance as they approached their home, greetings which would be followed by expectations of something worthwhile from their long time away.

Howard watched the faces of the men through the smudgy glass of the carriage. Their faces looked weather-beaten and tough. Men who had worked for every single morsel they had ever gotten since their birth. Some of them in their early twenties, an age where Howard could recall getting his first letter to work as an accountant right after he had finished his time in college. The young men before him were incapable of any literary activities and depended solely on their brute to get from day to day.

The ride from the train station took him through the lower town where the men from the last coach lived with their families. Dirt roads sprawled all across what many considered to be the underbelly of the society as log cabins littered the roadside. Many sold wares directly from their homes and some ran along the street with them, along with their kids. Mud puddles shook up his carriage as it plowed through the now-quiet streets. The rains had caused all activities to cease, but as Howard stared through the hazy glass, wiping the small fog his exhalation caused, he could see the flushed cheeks of children huddled together under a blanket waiting for the rains to cease so they could continue their business.

The dirt roads gave way to the paved cobblestone streets of Howard's neighborhood. He never truly felt comfortable leaving his home, as the discomfort from seeing the change in scenery always made him ask questions that those of his class considered a sacrilege. The houses furthest from his neighborhood looked as though they would fall apart anytime soon, but the closer he got to his home, the more the houses began to look like each other causing the transition from the slums to feel almost invisible. Well-painted and decorated, the houses in his neighborhood were simple yet designed with a taste for flair. Chimneys rose here and there, warming the bodies of the families that lived.

Howard paid the coachman, tipping him gratefully for getting him through his journey without too much trouble. The coachman walked him to his doorstep with an umbrella before returning to grab his briefcase and other bags. Howard thanked him and hauled his belongings through the front door of his home.

Howard Forsyth had lived in a smaller house in a more sequestered part of the town after college. His father had worked as a physician before his death, tending mostly to the upper elite of society. The Forsyths had earned themselves an upper hand because of this, as the folks of upper class requested their medical care to get to them faster and even more importantly with a manner of discretion that his father could offer, the payments only got as good at it could get. This allowed Howard and his father to move in closer to their customers, unquestioned and unbothered because everyone knew who his father was, they lived in a better part of town and the perks of their relationship with the people his father now treated was more than worth it. Right after his first job after college, his father passed away, leaving the family house to him.

The Forsyth household had five bedrooms, a grand hall, a study, and four conveniences. Each bedroom harbored a small chandelier that carried candles that were often the rooms' only source of light after daylight, and a number of mahogany furniture that sat, neatly arranged for the class they represented and the company they often welcomed. The walls were draped with wallpapers that masked the oddity of the wood, and paintings of different sizes by a variety of artists, which Howard and his father had collected over time, and the floors were made of some of the best of polished oak wood. Carpets imported from different parts of the world were spread out all across the house, giving it a lush cozy feeling.

The entire house was kept warm by the furnace in the end of the grand hall, slow-burning wood was being reduced to charred coal in the corner. To the left of the furnace was a large shelf, on display were the items which the Forsyth family had acquired over the years. Brass sculptures and figurines carved out of granite lined the shelves. Artifacts from Africa, West-Africa in particular, relics which Howard had learned their stories and knew better than some his own, because he'd not only learnt them for his curiosity and interest in the uniqueness of the man-made objects, but so he could have a tale to use to entertain the guests which they often had, a culture they'd learned as their family got closer to those of the upper class. A perfectly preserved skull of baby elephant hung to its side, tusks intact.

"Howard! You're back!"

"Yes, I am, Edmund. How have you been?"

Edmund Hall sat by the fireplace, a bit of scotch in one hand and a cigar in the other. He was a tiny man, about a foot shorter than Howard. Edmund got to his feet as he walked briskly over to him, a manner of movement that seemed odd for someone of that size, leaning his weight on the cane with which he walked. Howard found this surprising, but held his comments to himself. A firm handshake ensued between the two gentlemen.

"How was your meeting with Lord Palmerston?"

"Quite eventful, as you'd expect. He is quite the reputable fellow."

"Oh, that, I'm quite certain of. Where are my manners? You're back from your trip and I keep you on your feet? Please, retire to your chambers." Edmund tapped his cane on the floor hard twice, summoning one of the house servants. With a curt nod, Howard's bags were carried away. "I'll get one of them to run a bath for you. You must be exhausted from your travels. Now, go get some rest. I'll see you for dinner, yes?"

"Most certainly. Oh, and Edmund?"

"Yes, Howard?"

"Thank you."

The death of Howard's mother had thrown the Forsyth household into a dark period. Howard's Father cleared out all his servants and everything that would remind him of his late wife. This led to him working to keep his household in order, something he and Howard managed to do for decades. After his passing, Howard realized that he couldn't keep the house running on his own, not with his job dividing his attention. That was when he met Edmund.

Edmund Hall was a hustler, a man who had literally consciously bumped into Howard on the street, jumped into an apology and began to offer his sales of smoking pipes to the gentleman. When they first met, Howard was just finishing his education and Edmund was just another man from the outskirts of town looking to make a quick buck and move on to the next day. But Howard saw a different type of drive in Edmund. The man didn't just want his next meal, he wanted everything this life could offer and he was willing to do anything for it.

As Howard acquired the family house, Edmund quickly took the chance to let him know that it would be impossible to run such a large house on his own. Edmund, in turn, sought out the best servants from the lower town, getting them jobs in the Forsyth household. Getting his pay from Howard, he struggled to keep money in his pocket as it was easy to quickly see that his ultimate goal was to move up the social ladder and become a member of the elite society.

He spent his money buying clothes and items that he could flaunt out on the street, trying to appear higher than he was. He would attend balls and interact with those much higher than himself in the echelon of society. Whatever Edmund set his mind to, he would ensure the task was completed to perfection. Howard had grown quite fond of Edmund as he had come to respect the zeal of the man and his quest to become someone better and recognizable in the society.

"So, he seems happy with everything? I say that with the utmost inquisition as you are the only one for miles."

"Lord Palmerston doesn't exactly seem like a man who is easily pleased. Despite all my cajoling, he basically gave me nothing, just more work to do."

Edmund poured himself some more of the broth which they were having for supper, his mind working as he ate. He worked with Howard as his subordinate at the office, handling matters which were less pressing and could be done without the necessity of Forsyth overseeing them himself. "I'm guessing he wants you to oversee the new project at the steel mines?"

"Yes."

"Dammit."

"Watch your language, Edmund."

"But Sir…"

Howard held up a hand, causing Edmund to pause and recalibrate. "But Howard. The mines are under the jurisdiction of Sir Fitzhugh."

"And he in turn, reports to Lord Palmerston as well. If he tries to make a fuss, perhaps he would like to take his grievances straight to the Lord himself."

"It would be quite the undertaking." Edmund spoke with a mouthful of cabbage.

"It is a task I couldn't say no to. And maybe now, we might finally be able to move uptown with the profits from this."

"Well, yes, we may. It is just that I worry about Fitzhugh. That man is regarded notorious and as much as I would hate to say it, it would be quite a dangerous task."

A serving girl walked in, adding a large bowl of mutton to the table. Howard looked up at her, locking eyes. She smiled in return and did a little curt nod before backing away from the table. Edmund watched them between forkfuls of food, chewing inappropriately. As soon as she was out of earshot, Edmund cleared his throat.

"What would be truly dangerous, would be pursuing something with Adeline. It would do…"

"Edmund, let me worry about my social status. You have a lot of work to do as well. This is on both of us, I will be needing your help and we very much might be getting our hands dirty, so let us try to keep focused on the task, yes?"

"I'm not sure if I'm the one who lacks focus."

"Come again?"

"I'm just saying, if you truly aspire to move with the elite, the movers and shakers of this town, you can't be seen with the likes of Adeline, it's a hard truth. She is no doubt a nice lady, but for the sakes of your reputation and business, I highly suggest you to reconsider."

"I'll consider it."

The thunderstorm was at its peak after dinner. Howard retired to his bedroom, finding the doors to his quarters open. Adeline stood by a chair, her back to him as she folded his laundry, placing them into a wardrobe in front of her. She wore a long tan gown made mostly from animal hide and low-grade leather. The lights from the candles on the chandelier danced across her skin as the soft winds from the storm bothered them. She had long blonde hair tied into a single ponytail and tucked behind her to prevent it from getting in the way of her chores.

Howard remembered when he first met Adeline. Edmund had brought him a handful of young women who were looking to make a fair wage working in the Forsyth household. In the first week of her working there, Howard watched Adeline get in a fight with the servants already at work there, not backing down from men who were twice her size, trying to intimidate her with their masculinity. He admired her for her resolve and tenacity, and also for her beauty.

"Adeline."

She spun around at the sound of his voice, lightning lit up the night sky as she faced him, a burst of wind blew out a few candles.

"Master Forsyth."

They locked eyes for a moment as their minds reminisced in sync of all the times they had spent together and the time they had spent apart. The open door behind Howard prevented him from doing what he so dearly desired. In two steps, he would cover the distance between himself and Adeline, before lifting her in his arms into a tight embrace, locking their lips together in a primal hunger that would satiate both their desires.

The wind blew again, tugging lightly at the hem of her gown and at his collar. She drew her gaze away from him, turning to a nearby window and shut its louvers. She remained still, pretending to be busy fastening its lock. Adeline felt a shiver travel down her spine as Howard's hand ran down her cheek, causing her to turn a shade of red as a smile tugged at her face.

"Howard, we could… someone might see."

"Let them. I will not be a scared man in my own house."

"At least have the decency to shut the doors."

"I like to live dangerously." Howard spoke as he used the back of his leg to kick the door close.

"And just how dangerous would that be?" She spoke, joy filling her voice. She relaxed into his arms as he pulled her into a cuddle on the bed beside them.

"Dangerous enough... to do this... and this..." He kissed her on her neck and cheek, pausing midsentence for emphasis "...and stare death in the face every day. Just for you."

She stared at his face in the dim lighting of the room, not bothered about the candles which had gone off, which she was supposed to tend to. Her eyes searched his face as he returned the stare. There was nothing but pure and raw unabashed love etched into his face. Adeline felt this, as his hand pushed a loose strand of her hair to the side before planting another kiss, but this time on her lips.

They found comfort in each other's arms into the early hours of the morning. Adeline woke, greeted by the stare and smile of Howard.

"It will soon break dawn, I must leave."

"Must you?"

"Howard, you know I must. Someone here could see."

Howard let out a loud breath, he had woken earlier and busied himself daydreaming about what a life with the woman in his bed would be like. He knew the dangers it put him in if he was thought to be in bed with a woman from a different social standing as himself — a class that was considered purely irrelevant. His mind trembled at the few times he'd heard about and in fact secretly witnessed the execution of the romantic partners of those who worked for the lords, simply because they were of a low societal caste. One thing the Queen would not tolerate, was someone ruining her perfect segregation and echelon of society.

He worked for the state and reported to Lord Palmerston, and while he was middle class, there was still a chance that things could go very bad for them. But Howard thought maybe if he could work hard enough and get himself to be a part of the elite upper class, he could earn himself a voice that could maneuver the barricades of society and find a way to finally be with Adeline without fear. But until then, their love would have to be a secret, one that would remain behind locked doors and tightly drawn curtains.

A knock at the front door surprised them both. Howard heard the door being answered by Edmund from downstairs. He changed into a more respectful attire before coming down.

"Master Howard Forsyth." The man who had arrived stood and spoke on seeing Howard. "I, am Sir Archie Gilbert. Word has reached us at the mines that

Lord Palmerston has requested your services. Master Fitzhugh has requested that I and my men aid you in your commute to the mines today."

"A million thanks to Sir Fitzhugh, but I honestly don't think he should have made such a gesture. I'm sure your men would do more of a service there than here."

"Certainly, it was meant for your hospitality. Plus, we would like you to arrive there on time, the journey is such a tedious one by carriage."

Howard looked outside to see Fitzhugh's men waiting. "Let your men come inside, let us have breakfast while I ready myself for the journey. If the journey is as you say, I might need to pack a few things and I've never been to the mines. Let me offer you a drink, I have the very best liquor proffered from the Portuguese, I keep it only for my most honored guests. Besides, we auditors are known for our hospitality, and I must ensure that my guests feel most comfortable."

TWO

T he journey to the mines was one which Howard had never truly experienced before. He was fully aware of the feats of engineering the new power harnessed by the steam engines could. Archie and his men had arrived in vehicles that Edmund described as 'most peculiar.' They fit about three people and ran on a steam engine. They looked more like reverse chariots with their engines on their backsides, chugging and churning up steam and water. The forty-minute ride took them from the residential areas of the town to the mines on the outskirts.

A large crater had been carved in on a hillside. It was about three kilometers across and covered most of the surrounding area with vehicles similar in design to the one which they rode in. A set of rail lines crisscrossed the hillside, indicating where the first extracts were transferred to a train which would send it on to the steel mill to be processed. The morning sun rose over the mine, casting most of it into a shade from the surrounding hillside. Howard could see men down in the mines with pickaxes, going at the rock faces.

A loud explosion occurred on the far side of the mill as their vehicle got closer. Whatever had triggered the explosion had caused a landfall of one of the rock faces to the left of the mine. Rocks and dirt tumbled down loosely, bringing up a cloud of dust. There were a few buildings on the top of the hill, one of them was where the vehicle was stopped.

"This will be your office!" Archie spoke loudly, trying to speak over the sound of the steam engine vaporizing and condensing water multiple times per second. "I'll be back!"

He took off, the 'Steamcart' as they called it, zipped down into the mines, leaving a trail of dust behind it. Edmund picked up Howard's briefcase turning to the building. The structure was made out of bricks and concrete with a slate roof. It wasn't pretty, but it would hold well and defy the elements. Howard turned around to take in the scenery that was the mine. It was incredibly large, quite easy to lose a person down in it. He tried to find the steamcart that had brought him there but there were so many running around down in the mine, he gave up nearly instantly.

There were a few caves that seemed to be carved on the rings that led down around the edges of the mine into its center. The caves had little marks out in front, some of them had black paint with an X, and others were marked with dashes in red ink. Howard had never handled a project of this scale, just looking at it alone made him dizzy, but also buzz with excitement.

"There's nothing quite like it, is there?"

Howard was so caught up in the spectacle before him, he hadn't noticed the man who stood beside him make his way there until he spoke. He instantly recognized the voice from his time in the town square. Fitzhugh White, the man in charge of running the mines. He was a little taller than Howard, and a lot broader from the shoulders too. His shirt seemed to be holding back a hulking mass of pure muscle. Built most likely from his time in the Queen's army or his time in the mines here.

Fitzhugh was originally a soldier recruited personally into the private armies of Lord John Russell. They had joined the battle against the Qing dynasty and given the battle their all. Fitzhugh was sent home after a support beam from one of the warring ships broke loose and shattered his left leg from the shin. After years in rehabilitation, he was given command over governing the mines as a temporary replacement until whoever was in charge then would return. His body might have no longer been fit to go to war but his mind was still that of a stern soldier. And as it so happened, the man in charge of the mines never returned as it was learnt that he died of very questionable events.

"Never have I seen anything of this manner in my travels."

"Then I suggest you travel some more, Sir Howard. I hear the gold mines of the west are nearly twelve times as large as this one."

"Which must make handling its affairs a serious issue. But gladly, you have me."

"Yes" He turned to face Howard, extending his hand to shake, "Yes we do."

The handshake was warm and fierce, Howard could tell instantly the difference between their hands and their grips; his being the gentle grip of a man that hadn't toiled a quarter of what Fitzhugh had for his hand to feel so hard and seemingly impermeable. He felt a certain level of tension just by standing next to Fitzhugh. Fitzhugh was intimidating even when he did not mean to be, because he was a man who was considered notorious for getting obstacles out of his way quickly and efficiently. Howard had every right to be wary of him; the man had his own small private army, one which he bragged often about arming them himself.

"Is it always like this down here?"

"I think you mean up here. Where we stand here, it is considered *up*. Down there in the mines? Most likely, yes. Every single day all year round. We have to continue to provide the Queen's men with the metal they need to make more inventions, build more ships. Have you seen the marvelous things they have done with this steam energy? I believe this thing will revolutionize the colonies."

"As long as we play our part."

"Yes, as long as we do. I believe you've seen your office?"

"I haven't been inside it yet."

"Well, unpack your bags and get used to the space. I would like to give you a personal tour of the mines before it is high noon, so maybe you would begin your work." Fitzhugh made a loud whistling sound and a steamcart drove up to his side with its driver waiting on his command. "I need you to find Archie, tell him to ready the caves, we're moving ahead with that." He spoke to the worker beside him who hurried off looking to pass the message.

"I will be a few moments." Howard called as he got into the office, seeing Edmund already placing down his files and trying to get the dust off most of the furniture. The space seemed cramped with just the two men in it, something that bothered Howard as he was a big fan of his own space.

"Was that Fitzhugh?"

"Yes."

"What did he say to you?" Edmund asked with a slight tremble in his voice.

"It is just as I feared, Edmund. He's asked me to relocate to the mines fully, we're not going to make it home today my friend."

Edmund stared with wide eyes as his brain scrambled to figure out the comedic tone of the sentence.

"Oh relax, he offered to give me a tour of the mine. I think it would be best if we bot…"

Another explosion rattled the building. This one was accompanied by loud voices outside screaming something incoherent. The two men exchanged glances.

"That's normal, right?"

The screaming escalated causing both men to run outside. A large plume of dust hung in the air, wafted back and forth by the gentle spring winds. Howard and Edmund stared down into the mine, unable to tell what had happened. Howard looked around for the closest worker he could find, grabbing him by the shoulder.

"What is going on?"

"One of the caves collapsed! We have men stuck in there and the reservoir…"

A large steel structure that was designed for holding and transferring water around the mill which sat a few yards from each cave. The water mostly served for powering the machines that drilled the holes but now the one next to the cave which had collapsed had toppled over and begun pouring into the cave. There was no other outlet for any of the caves as they were one-way openings, so the water would pour into the hole until it filled it up, drowning the men inside.

Howard took off running towards the scene of the incident. He was over five hundred meters away and unsure of what to do when he would arrive at the cave, but he carried on, Edmund following nimbly behind.

Between the dust and commotion, Howard saw Fitz-hugh standing in front of the collapsed cave. He stood there, staring at the rubble in front of its opening, a sight that stunned and confused Howard. Archie suddenly appeared next to him in a slightly larger steamcart, this one was hauling a lot more than just a man.

Archie heaved the large pieces of equipment which he had brought in on the vehicle. Separated, they made no sense to Howard, but slowly as Archie and a few others helped assemble it onto Fitzhugh, it started to make some sense. It wrapped around his body with large boots that easily made him nearly nine feet tall. It had a large vest in the midsection, behind it seemed to be the engine that powered the machine. On his arms were large glove-like arms. The one on the right hand was equipped with a large base and about four smaller vices which worked like fingers and the left hand seemed to just be a plain metal sheet.

The entire thing looked like it weighed a ton, as Howard tried to comprehend — aside from how he had managed to obtain the machine — how Fitzhugh was able to carry the entire weight of the monstrosity, but then he could see the plethora of pistons and gears peaking in and out of the midsection. The part that wrapped around Fitzhugh's torso held the entire thing together, complete with the steam engine, all strapped together. The sound coming from it was loud and ear splitting, the metal parts whirring and the engine working overtime to keep the machine upright. Howard and Edmund took a step back, watching in complete awe.

Fitzhugh turned around, facing the cave's entrance and threw his left hand, in the direction of the rock. The machine's left arm followed suit, punching deep into the rock, throwing smaller pieces around. Two large copper beams were quickly attached underneath as the men worked feverishly, in a manner that seemed almost rehearsed. The beams would give the mechanical arm support, something it needed as the flat end of it already buried in the rock fired the metal sheet deeper into the caves entrance. This flat surface held up a significant portion of rubble that would come tumbling down if the ones blocking up the cave's entrance were to escape.

Water had begun gathering around the feet on the machine and the men standing around it. Fitzhugh bent the other arm downward, using the vices to pull out large boulders and pieces of rocks. As he carried out this action, more rocks fell loose from the top, pouring straight on the copper beam and arm of the machine holding up the top of the cave. The water around his feet rushing into the cave as he paved a way open for the men trapped in. Once the space he had dug out was wide enough, a hand shot through it, open and facing up as though whoever owned it was begging for assistance. Edmund grabbed onto Howard, stricken with fear. Fitzhugh worked faster, pulling and pulling away from the collapsed cave until finally a man fell out, sputtering and coughing from the water that had nearly drowned them.

Six men were pulled out of the cave, none of them seriously injured thanks to the pre-planned precautions taken by the mines. But without the help from Fitzhugh, the men would be as good as dead.

"I'm sorry about earlier this morning, Mr. Forsyth. The mines can be a treacherous place, and even our most prepared contingencies will almost always have some loop in them."

Fitzhugh was meeting with Howard a few hours after the incident. He had cleaned up and changed into a more formal three-piece suit; the dirt and the filth of the troubles they had just witnessed at the mines appearing nowhere on him. Howard noticed he carried a pistol with him, tucked slightly underneath his coat, not much attempt made to hide it. Fitzhugh loved being feared and would take to anything that would continue to propagate that.

"It's alright. The men, how are they doing?"

"Quite fine, considering. I mean, a few broken bones and terrified lungs, but nothing that a lot of rest won't fix."

Howard nodded, uncomfortable being in the same room as a man with so many stories of his past being so vile and diabolical.

"I just can't help but say; the machine, the one you used to help them. That was quite an incredible piece of machinery, quite a sight to behold, I've never seen anything like that."

"Ah, yes, of course, one of the wonders of steam power."

"How, might I ask, did you come about it?"

"Come about it? Oh, no. See, I and my men made that beauty with our bare hands. Crafted from the very metal we get here from the mines. We consider it to be the future of mankind. I call it *The Coroner*."

The tales of his time in the army came into Howard's mind as the man uttered the words. Most particularly now, the rumors of how Fitzhugh had once taken the name 'Coroner'. One that told, that on a special secret mission behind enemy lines, Fitzhugh was said to have infiltrated a naval command ship of the Qing dynasty. That on getting aboard the ship, he slaughtered everyone on board singlehandedly.

Taking the lives of crew members and soldiers of an opposing army was one thing, but on investigation, it turned out that the ship was actually one which had rescued women and children captured by Queen Victoria's army that were being taken back to China. Fitzhugh didn't spare a single one of them. No one knew for sure how many were aboard the ship, as he sank the vessel after murdering them all. He was never tried for war crimes, as a matter of fact, his actions gained him favor in the eyes of a handful of lords working with the Queen.

Granted command of his own small battalion, he was allowed freedom to move around the entire empire, carrying out executions of those who dared to stand against the Queen and her men. A conflict of interest between two lords had resulted in the ousting of Fitzhugh. He was placed under the watch of Lord Palmerston as his previous crimes were quickly swept under the rug, allowing him to restart. Lord Palmerston knew of the stories and what Fitzhugh was capable of, the reports had reached him firsthand form his superiors. His repute by his unfortunate accident meant he would restrict Fitzhugh to the mines to ensure he would never become the man he once was.

"Is there a problem?"

"Not at all, Sir Fitzhugh." Howard turned to leave the room.

"Forsyth. Please, call me Fitz."

The tone sounded a bit too informal. Something which was incredibly out of character for a man with his history. Howard turned on his heel with a curt nod. "Fitz."

"There is something else I would like to discuss with you."

"And what would that be?"

"Well, as you can see the mines are certainly no place for, well, it's not really safe. I have the safety of my men to look after and while I respect Palmerston's directive, I do believe it would be best if you could work, perhaps off site?"

"Why so? Here, I can keep an eye on things better. And I am quite capable of taking care of myself."

"And I'm certain you can. But as you've already seen, accidents happen here, and it's quite impossible to tell what could happen to who, or when it could. It only makes sense to do all that is possible to avoid whatever casualties might become, and that includes having only the most essential personnel at the site."

"I'll send Sir Edmund home and only bring him with me when it is of utmost importance. I'm sure these accidents don't happen everyday?"

"No."

"Then I'm certain we won't have the bottom of the jar's luck."

Fitzhugh ground his jaw and released a fist Howard didn't see him make. He obviously didn't like to be challenged, and he hoped that that would be the end of it.

"Well then, I do hope we can all work perfectly together."

"I'm sure we can." Howard tipped his hat in his direction before turning off.

"Terribly sorry, I keep cutting you off. Would you mind if maybe I could ask you a small favor? Well, you see, due to the incident with the cave now, we're a bit short staffed, but Lord Palmerston will still be expecting his steel to reach him. By the turn of the week, we have a train which shuttles it all the way down to the coast where it will be loaded up to the ships and taken out to him. Perhaps you could help accompany the train?"

"Of course." Howard stared at him, obliging without considering it for a moment. Then a thought occurred to him. "I believe I have a request of my own. Just an art of the trade. Is there any way I can gain access to the previous files of whoever audited here?"

"I'm afraid that will be impossible. You're the first auditor we're going to have, the only personnel we've had is an accountant and I don't think…"

"Oh no, that's more than fine. I just need something to give me a foot in the door. If you can get someone to hand in the file before sundown?"

"By sundown? Well I don't that will be entirely be possible either. See, our previous accountant no longer works here as you know. He moved everything he had, office included, to his home in town."

"Then I think I will be able to get it from him on my way home."

The two men stood facing each other for a few moments, Howard unsure of what course of action to take. He was quite certain he had gotten on the nerves of Fitzhugh by being so unyielding, and he had little idea as to how he might deescalate the situation. A bead of sweat had formed on the eyebrow of the former soldier, his eyes remaining unnervingly calm, but his head was moving so quickly it seemed it wasn't, he was calculating.

Howard Forsyth was a problem, this, Fitzhugh knew even before the man had been called to work with him, but now he was seeming more than Fitzhugh had bargained for, and such problems always affected his plans. But as always, he knew just how to solve problems, he considered himself a professional at tackling issues and this would be no different. The auditor would have to be taken care of as quickly and discreetly as possible, and then, his plan could continue.

"I'll have someone send up his address to you. Have a nice day Sir Forsyth, welcome to the mines."

He walked past Howard, letting their shoulders brush against each other lightly. It was such a soft tap, Howard couldn't tell if it was an antagonistic gesture, but one thing was clear to him. Fitzhugh did not like him being around.

THREE

A deline picked up a white cotton towel from the floor of the bedroom. The late afternoon sun poured into the room in slants through the steel bars of a window as dust mites danced around. The room smelled of lavender and goat milk, two substances which had just been used on the child sitting on the bed. Adeline watched after him occasionally for additional income, a job she was not quite fond of just yet.

"I'm leaving now." A call came from the adjoining room, the mother of the child. A woman of the elite class, too occupied to look after her own young, as having tea was a more pressing matter.

"Yes, mistress."

She walked into the room, giving Adeline a once over and then turning to find her son sitting on the bed. She wore her makeup heavily and carried a large purse, one without a handle. It was something Adeline couldn't understand. Her own purse always had a handle, so it would aid her in grasping it. She thought perhaps it was another of the subtle gestures by ladies of the elite class, doing everything they could to set themselves apart from the commoners, the women of the foot class of the colonies, the ones that wore dresses they wouldn't be caught dead in. To ladies like the mistress, almost everything meant power. It was laced in the very air they breathed — as they surely had been taught right before they could define what exactly power meant or pronounce the word without infancy in their tone. The nuances of their lives had been morphed around carrying themselves to suit appreciation, from the softness in their gait, the soundlessness that must be in their laughters, to the fragrance that traveled with them, and now down to the manner of purses they carried. Class looked to Adeline to be something short of a mental illness.

"When you put him to bed, be sure to leave the premises and come find me at the stable. If I'm not there by then, then I suggest you return tomorrow. Then you can get your pay."

"Yes mistress." Adeline repeated, trying not to keep eye contact with her.

"Oh, and Tom?" She called out to her son. "If she does anything wrong, do try to tell me when I return, alright?"

"Yes mama."

She left Adeline standing in suppressed rage. The help fought the negative thoughts that came rushing into her mind as there was so much she could do, but she thought against it. She turned to face the child.

"Alright Tom, time for bed."

"No! Not yet..."

"Yes, Tom, I have to get going. You need to go to bed right this instant, young man."

"But I want a story!"

"Tom."

"Please… Adeline. Just one?"

She let out a labored breath, staring at the child with pleading eyes. He would be groomed in the ways of his parents, most likely his father and would grow up to inherit a fortune and learn the trade of the men before him. Another arrogant uptown folk who cared nothing for the likes of herself. But right there in that very moment where he stared at her pleading, all she could see was a child who wanted a good tale.

"Alright, Tom. I think I have one story for you, and this one is a true story, and very few people know about it. Now, get under the covers so I can begin, will you?" She shut the window louvers, cutting off most of the light entering the room as the boy agreed to her request, eager and innocent for her story.

"Long before you were born, when the queen was about my age in fact, there was a man called Jeffery. He was a soldier, a man of valor and courage who gave all for the Queen and for country. One day, on one of his missions, Jeffery found something."

"Was it a magic sword?"

"No Tom. Le—"

"The Loch Ness monster?"

"Don't be naughty, no. No interruptions Tom, or else…" She trailed off for a second and continued, "Now, Jeffrey found something much more powerful than that. He found love. And that love, he found in the form of a woman named Samantha."

Adeline paused, staring at a space behind Tom fixatedly as she felt the memories of all the times the story was narrated to her. "Now, Samantha was an amazing woman. The very first to ever capture the heart of Jeffery. She was unlike anyone he had ever met and he knew that Samantha was the one he would make his wife. But there was a problem. She was from the colonies. A poor family from the south without a single claim to their name. The Queen forbade her men to have anything to do with these southerners, or even people of lower class themselves as she felt it would blur the lines of power. But she was blind to the lines of love.

Jeffrey and Samantha secretly kept seeing each other under the cover of darkness, afraid to be seen by anyone, praying for some miracle that would allow them both to be together. But then, things rarely ever work out perfectly in this world. Someone found out about them and their little secret and had it reported to a very mean man called Lord Carrington. He was a very bad man and he did a lot of bad things."

"Was he a real lord?" Tom asked between a yawn.

"Oh yes, he was. Very much real. And when he found out about Jeffery and Samantha, he caught them and gave a very nasty order to Jeffery. He asked him to kill Samantha himself, to prove he did not care for her. But Jeffery could not, he refused to do so, disobeying an order from a lord. Carrington became very furious as well, he felt insulted, but Jeffery was still a soldier of the Queen, so, looking for the ultimate way to punish Jeffery, Carrington took his horse and set on the journey himself. He would ride to the Queen herself and let her know of Jeffrey's disobedience. If the Queen knew, Samantha would be killed by the Queen's order and Jeffery would most likely be sent home from the army and stripped of his rank.

"Jeffery learnt of his lord's plan and knew he couldn't let Samantha die, so off he went after Carrington with his horse. Jeffery rode much faster than his lord, and so he caught up with him long before they got anywhere near the Queen's palace. After a long and grueling fight, Jeffery managed to take down Lord Carrington, but by doing so, the soldier of valor became an enemy of the state. That night, he sought after Samantha and left her with a single message: to leave the state and never return. Days later, Jeffery was caught and hung for high treason.

"Samantha escaped, pregnant with a child which she had for him. They settled down somewhere on the plains of Greene County."

"You mean Samantha is here?"

"No, Tom. She is long dead, bless her soul. But her child is somewhere here among us, waiting for a chance."

"To do what?"

"To change it all. To take down the Queen and her silly rules of who gets to be with who and how she needs things to be organized. One day, hopefully, Samantha's child will get that chance and commoners will be able to eat every and any dish they wished and would have the freedom to love whoever they pleased."

Tom fell quiet, his eyebrows creased deep in thought. Adeline noticed that she had most likely scared the child and given him thoughts which would be overbearing for his young mind. He might grow up to be another entitled man that trotted the colonies and oppressed the lower class, but he was still very much a child that had only wanted a bedtime story, and she saw him as nothing other than that when she told him the tale.

The innocence in the child's eyes had been what made her leave out the worst of what Samantha's child would go through after she was born. Adeline did not tell the child about the how Samantha had died of a mysterious illness because the closest physician to the south had moved a week's journey away, further into the colonies, closer to the center of the state where it would be almost impossible for the residents of the south to reach, at least not if they needed the help urgently. Adeline had left out how Samantha's child, at just five years of age, had sat beside her mother where she laid in her dying bed and withered in spite all the efforts of the neighbors. She'd left out how Samantha's daughter had to be pried away from her hands when days passed and the woman did not fare any better, when people feared what she had might become something that spread and infect her daughter and the rest of the town. Adeline had left out the fact that Samantha had died the day after she was separated from her daughter, and she was buried in an unmarked grave far away from where they lived because there was no one to tell them otherwise, and no one would save them or their children if they fell ill so mysteriously too.

Adeline kept Tom ignorant of how Samantha's child would grow without her mother and father, in the south where families already had more than enough of themselves to worry about when it came to matters of feeding and survival, so that they would only be kind to the child if she was willing to labor for a portion of stale bread and cold soup. She did not mention that the child had begun to sleep in people's barns and stables after the landlord took over their house. That Samantha's child had woken up many nights in the winter, freezing as death, and calling for her mother till she would remember that her mother was no more, and the child would crawl back in the corner of the barn where the pigs hadn't already shit and the hay was the warmest.

And she would weep till her voice lost its strength, she would weep herself to sleep, she would sleep without a mother, without a father, without a help to tell her stories and comfort her cold hands and feet.

Samantha's daughter would survive doing everything she could. No task would seem too unworthy for her, not someone of her class, not a girl child with no family. She would grow with a company of friends that had a similar fate as she did, and she would learn the art of survival from them in many ways. They would teach her tricks that should naturally have been unheard of for a young lady, and she would defy their taunts and pull off those tricks even better than they ever did. The girl would often pack her hair tight under a cap and bask herself in boy's cloths, rags, whenever her gang were out testing out their new tricks or just using the old ones to get themselves food for the day. There would be a time when those tricks wouldn't help and the girl and her friends would go nights on end without food in their bellies. And they would have to beg, something the girl detested with the deepest part of her heart, but she would do it nevertheless. The girl and her friends would leave the town and go to the roads where they could encounter travelers that stopped and they would ask these well-dressed and well-spoken people for whatever it is they could kindly spare for them. Some would toss half-eaten breads at them, some would be kind enough to offer the kids the phlegm of their throats and words that broke the kids' hearts even more, and on a very fair day they would encounter a lord's son that tossed them a penny as his father's carriage drove by and he peeked through the window with a smile on his face.

When this girl turned fifteen, she would find a Madam Saleh, a lady who knew how to get southerners to the houses of the elites where they could work as handmaids, helps, stablemen, cooks and be whatever it is that the masters and mistresses needed. She would beg Madam Saleh to get her a job, and the lady would ask her if she had any skills that did not include cutting corners, one that perhaps involved the care of a home. The girl would shake her head and Madam Saleh would offer that the girl stayed with her instead, so that she could learn how to do the things the helps that worked in the bigger houses did, and so that she would have food in her belly and a warm corner to lay when the night got too cold. And the girl would accept.

Adeline looked at Tom as the boy slept without bother, the candles of the chandelier in the room burning with their dancing flames that lit it up in the absence of any daylight. She watched the kid as he slept in a bed of his own, in a room of his own, in a house his father owned and she saw the opposite of what she had had, what she wished she had had, and what she would have had had the Queen not taken it away by being so evil as to hating on people of the lower class so much that it became a sin in the state for people of middle and elite class to associate with them let alone have them as lovers. Adeline watched as the boy let out a little snore through his pebble-like nose and she remembered why she would do whatever she could so that the absurd declaration that had ruled her life would come to an end. When she tore her face away from the child and came to herself again, she remembered the mistress had asked her to be at the stable once the child was asleep, and she got out from beside the child's bed and found her away down the stairs, hoping she wouldn't have to wait till the next day to get paid.

The home of Bryce Allen was a grand work of architecture. One of the finer houses of the Middle class. Howard had known the name of the man who claimed ownership of the household, but their paths had never crossed. Even within the middle circle of society, there were those who were in a serious struggle to cross over to the highest levels of society and thus, they barely had much to do with their fellows. The house was littered with windows and verandas. The flags jutting out left and right made the building seem a bit chauvinistic but then, the man who lived there was one of the few people to ever be graced by the presence of the Queen herself.

As Howard approached from the courtyard, admiring the perfectly tended garden it sported he noticed the building had three chimneys. His mind quickly rushed back to the winter periods and he realized that he had only ever seen one smoking. He smiled in confirmation, houses with more chimneys were considered to belong to wealthier men. Some had gone as far as building fake chimneys into their roofs. He noticed a young man dressed in a two-piece black and white uniform waiting for him at the door. He stood upright, sizing him up.

"Hello there!" Howard called out to him with a wave of his cane. "Howard Forsyth. I would like to see Master Allen Here."

"Master Forsyth." The servant spoke with a well-toned voice and with an etiquette that seemed incredibly uncanny for the average individual. "I'm afraid Master Allen cannot see you now. Perhaps I shall inform him that you came, and you may return another time."

"I can't have that. I need to see him this instant, as it is of utmost importance." Howard didn't break eye contact as he spoke with the servant. "If you must, tell him I've been sent from the mines by Sir Fitzhugh."

The servant's eyes popped at the sound of the name, obviously recognizing it. "I shall ask him to reconsider. Do come in."

He was allowed into the building, one not too distinct from his. Its entrance also had a hall, but this was nearly twice as large as his. The single working chimney roared right before him, consuming wood. The walls were lined with wooden masks, relics and objects he had likely acquired from a sale of items brought home from the African colonies. Howard was given a plush oak chair to sit in while he waited. The servant disappeared into one of the doorways, leaving him alone.

Howard found it unsettling as to how an accountant had amassed enough wealth to procure a home so grand and lavishly furnished. Perhaps Bryce Allen had another occupation which paid better than accountancy. Whatever it was, Howard was hoping to get him to divulge some trade secrets, also and perhaps most importantly, a few tips as to how to handle working with Fitzhugh.

He walked across the hall on seeing the study of the accountant on the other end of the building. Its double doors left open in an almost welcoming manner. Behind the large desk was a shelf, packed with books and documents calling out to him. Howard found himself inside the study, his finger running over the books, studying their names for one which would pique his interest.

"They're my most treasured possessions."

Howard gripped on his cane tightly as the voice pulled him out of his self-imposed utopia. It took a second to regain his composure, before he turned around. "They are absolutely amazing, Master Bryce."

"Forsyth." He said the name as though it was a new flavor which he tasted. Bryce Allen was an older man who had come to rely heavily on his cane. "Nicholas Forsyth. You're his boy. How goes it?"

"Very well, my good sir. I see you've kept with the times. These pieces on the wall, the masks and relics. They must've cost a fortune." Howard gestured to the wooden masks which hung on the walls of his study.

"I spent most of my income buying off pieces of history. That's what my wife called it, bless her soul. At first, she used to think I was crazy, but now I do believe I have the largest collection of the African culture in the entire South, the queen herself commended that."

"I'm quite sure she did. It must have been a thrill of a lifetime, I'm certain."

"Oh, it was. I believe I met your father a few days prior to that even. He had to come down and give me a once over making sure that I was in perfect health and would not be doing anything, unconsciously, to put the Queen in harm's way. A necessity in this day and age. The town talked about it for months on end."

"Truly. We all did."

"Shall I offer you a drink? Scotch? Brandy?"

"Whatever you please, Sir Bryce."

The servant went to work with a wave of a wrist, reappearing with a tray and two glasses in them along with a bottle of the golden-brown liquor, balanced precariously on the forearm of the butler. He set down the tray and flipped the cups over, offering to pour. Allen waved him down, insisting on doing it himself.

"I believe this was distilled over sixteen years ago." He took a sip out of his own glass, nodded in approval and proceeded to let it flow into both cups to a reasonable amount. Both men lifted their glasses and drank nearly half its contents in a single gulp, fighting the burning sensation that made their eyes water.

"Impeccable."

"I concur. So, what brings you to my home? I'm sure a man of your caliber did not come all this way to simply talk about art and share a drink with an old man."

"A well-aged man."

"Flatter me all you will, Forsyth, but we both know we're well past small talk."

"Yes. We are. I'm here on behalf of Lord Palmerston, I have been tasked with performing audits on the mines under the jurisdiction of Sir Fitzhugh."

The older man froze at the mention of the name. He dropped his glass on the table, locking eyes with Howard as though he had just said something extremely insulting. "I see."

"Yes, I was hoping that perhaps I could get my hands on the documents, the ledger you had while you worked with Fitzhugh, as they are of supreme importance and would be of immeasurable help with my work. And maybe, if I could get some advice as to working with him, considering you've done a lot of that in the past."

Bryce lifted his thumb and index finger to the bridge of his nose, rubbing it lightly as though what Howard had said were making him light headed. On returning his hand to the side, it knocked over his glass, throwing it to the polished wooden floor and smashing the ware to bits. He mumbled under his breath as the butler got to work before he had to be called, making the incident disappear. Howard realized that the older man was waiting, looking around nervously as though the entire room itself were listening in on their conversation.

"Forsyth." He spoke in hushed tones as soon as the servant left to dispose the glass, so close to him that he could smell the alcohol on his breath and see the crow's feet etched into the corners of his eyes. He could see the creases and wrinkles that crisscrossed his skin, dancing along. "Your father was a smart man, I'm sure he raised a smart boy as well. You do not want to do this."

"I'm sure I don't know what you mean…"

"Surely, you're no fool, even if you've never associated with the man, you must have some idea about how dangerous Fitzhugh is. I cannot think of a man in Greene County that doesn't. You want the ledger? You can have it; I'd be more than happy to part with it and be over with Fitz and his dealings. I've had enough to do with them, but you should be the wiser. Fitzhugh is not a man you can take lightly. People don't stand in his way and have it easy. He gets what he wants and there is nothing to be done about that."

"I have no fear of Fitzhugh."

"Then perhaps I misspoke earlier and you're a fool after all." Bryce turned to his table and fiddled with a key on the lowest drawer, retrieving a thick ledger, about 200 pages thick. "I would ask you to give this a second thought, but if indeed you know what he is capable of and you still choose to meddle, then perhaps there is no saving you." He looked at the ledger one last time and handed it over to his guest, "Be careful, Forsyth. Fitz is not a man to be played with. Now, if you don't mind, I will need you to leave my house."

FOUR

E dmund sat by a candle stand, on a chair in the main room with his unlit cigar trapped between his lips as he held a newspaper in his hands and stared at it with seriousness in his eyes. The newspapers came in weekly into the town from the big printing press and news house up in the County and he'd made it a habit to read them whenever they arrived. It was — like every other thing the man had been doing lately — an effort to get himself recognized as a man of a class that was fit to sit with the lords at tables where they discussed matters of intellect and social importance. He read the news to keep himself apprised and so he appeared updated whenever he spoke or added to a conversation, he also took his time at the words to better whatever parts of his vocabulary might be lacking, and it had been working quite well for him.

He sat and studied the paper, pausing between reads every few minutes to take a sip of the scotch in the glass on the footstool by his side, which meant he would have to take the unlit roll of tobacco out from his mouth each time as he worked with one hand, and he continued the process till he heard the front door open and Adeline walked in with her satchel across her body. He directed his gaze to her and their eyes met where she stood for a moment and gave the man a curt nod before she headed to the kitchen.

She walked away and he watched her till she disappeared into the chamber, and he remembered how he'd come about her so that she would become one of the helps he got for Howard Forsyth. He had asked for the very best and madam Saleh had sung Adeline's praise like he'd never heard anyone sing a help's praise before, and he had agreed they would employ the young lady with the only clause being that she would be treated with no lesser respect than they would treat another human being. Adeline was yet to fail in regard of the things that her previous mistress had praised her, but now he worried furtively at the other thing she had gotten into that must not leave the walls of the house. The young lady was fair and a pleasure to behold no doubt, and her background and class might be irrelevant to the society, but what she lacked in status and wealth and quality of acquaintance, she made up for with her looks and dexterity in and out of the kitchen. But the things he knew about her, the things many others knew about her would unfortunately not be able to save her from the wrath of the Queen and her counsel if ever word left the walls of the house about the services she offered her master after hours, the way she looked at him and he did her. Edmund feared more than anything what trouble the game the two were playing would bring upon the house, upon Howard, and what would become of himself and the relationships he'd been trying so hard to build. He cared greatly for his presence amidst the elite, but it was undeniable that he owed his rise in the past years to his relationship with Howard which had earned the man his loyalty. Edmund Hill hence was trapped in doing whatever he could to make sure knowledge of the forbidden romance never made it past the three of them.

Adeline wasted no time before she got to her duties at the kitchen, assisting the other helpers as they prepared for the next morning. Although she would never make it obvious, deep down, she was really still struggling, and telling her life story to that child had only dug up more memories and feelings she had been trying to get over. There were nights when she would jerk awake from the lingering fear, and the terror that followed her mother's demise. She still hated sleeping in the cold and the smell of pork still troubled her. She had wanted to be mad at the folks that buried her mother so far away, but then she'd gotten older and began to see their fears for the reality that they were. The sight of her mother's ail body lying on the bed in their home was etched in the back of her mind still, she could not let it go; she did not know if she really wanted to, it was the last time she'd seen her and she feared if she let herself forget she would not remember what her mother looked like anymore.

Growing up in the southern colonies was a challenge on its own, but surviving as an orphan with no family was a feat not many people could boast of having achieved, bur she had, and she could, barely. Before she set out to find madam Saleh, she'd watched Thomas, the biggest kid of their misfit gang of three, get taken away by the Queen's soldiers for recruitments that probably had nothing to do with the army. Thomas had been seventeen for almost eight months but they'd kept telling everyone that ever bothered to ask that he was still sixteen, because the soldiers were allowed to raid the south colonies of their seventeen-year-old boys who were already men, to have them serve the Queen.

There were rumors of what happened to the boys and what they were made to do in the company of the army, but no one in the southern colonies knew for sure, as none of the boys taken that way ever made it back to tell the tale. Now, when families had sons close to the age, they would send them far away with their fathers and other men for years on end, so they could learn to work with their hands and be safe, and someday come home when the soldiers could no longer take them without questions.

They might not have known what happened to Thomas after he was taken, but she knew what became of the only other relationship she had then, as it was taken apart again in the name of the Queen.

Madam Saleh promised she would teach her what she needed to know about caring for a home, and the woman kept to her word. Adeline could handle an entire house from start to finish before she broke a sweat, she could make meals the likes that would make lords and ladies bite their tongues and savor for more. She'd learned from the very best and it paid off where she found herself now.

When Edmund mentioned she was going to be serving Howard Forsyth, she'd kept her mind open and her thoughts frozen at the idea of finally being a help to a man of some class; she'd heard stories from other helps that had returned from their services to different lords, mistresses and masters, and they were hardly ever ones that warmed the heart or brought confidence. Which was why when she finally met Howard in person and discovered the kind of heart he carried in his chest was not like any she'd heard of, she did not know what to make of him.

She'd only ever done her duties in the house without reproach, but even when she thought perhaps, he might find some wrong in the way she did something, he held back. And she found herself filled with all manner of feelings for her master as she became even more comfortable around him with every passing day. She noticed soon enough that the man stole glances at her when he thought no one was looking, at first, she'd thought it inappropriate as she remembered the stories some helps had told at madam Saleh's. But Howard Forsyth was a fine, fine man, and a gentleman like she'd never known. So, she watched as his glances continued, often consciously putting herself in his view, till she could make him know that she'd caught his stolen glances.

Now, Adeline carried a stack of towels up to her master's room, eager for him to take her in his arms and make her feel warm, even if it would be just for the night. She treaded gently towards the door, hoping to leave behind the terror of her mother's dying face and the doom that only ever accompanied the thought of the Queen and her rule. She felt it heavy in her heart the thought that the name might again strike on her life and take away something she cared about, something she loved. But she said nothing as she landed a gentle knock on Howard's door and let herself in.

Nicholas Forsyth was a physician that knew his trade, and even better, he was a man that knew how to talk to people when it seemed like the situation might be a lost cause, an undeniably vital skill for a man of his profession to have, and it earned him more than just the respect of the people he treated, it often brought him material forms of appreciation from them and their acquaintances. Such was the large Magolini desk that stole the spotlight from every other thing in his study, where it sat right in the center, with light from the chandelier hanging in the study and the lamp on top of the desk doing their best to cast reflections off the polished furniture, and leaving its shadow as a thick presence where they couldn't reach.

Lord Birmingham's new wife, Jolene, had been in been in labor for over twelve hours and was yet to show any signs of letting out the baby in her belly. The mid-wives had exhausted all they could for the woman and yet nothing changed, so the unsettled lord sent word to Howard's father who arrived the quickest he could, examined the woman and determined that the child needed to be taken out as quickly as possible or both it and the mother would not see the light of the coming day. Lord Birmingham had almost collapsed at the words, as the man had only lost his first wife less than a year before, but Nicholas Forsyth was a physician that was gifted, he had performed the Cesarean Section a handful of times before, and only ever lost a patient who had developed a rare complication. So, he talked to Birmingham like a man, and a trained physician that he was, and made him see reason quickly.

The procedure lasted over three hours, but the physician emerged with the agile newborn in his hands and the mother alive. And Lord Birmingham would become more than grateful.

His father had had a smaller mahogany desk in his study, and he had it moved to the master bedroom to make room for Lord Birmingham's exquisite gift. Now Howard sat at the desk with his shirt loosened to reveal the small collection of hair on his chest, as he scanned keenly at the documents in front of him through the dim lights, wondering if perhaps Bryce Allen had handed him the wrong papers by any chance.

He picked up one of the documents that comprised the ledger the former accountant of the mines had given him, and he inspected the details on it closer, leaning towards the lamp on his right, feeling perhaps the stress of the eventful day at the mines and his unscheduled detour was getting to hi. But it wasn't, the auditor had a perfect vision and what he was seeing simply could not have been right. He held the document in his hand while his mind worked at the possibilities, just as a knock landed on the door and peeled him away from the discovery.

"Yes, enter."

Adeline opened the door gently and smiled at the knowledge of his solitude in the room. "I've been up to your chambers, master. I did not find you there."

"I've been here since I returned. I'm sorry for the trouble, I just have something pressing facing me right now, and I'm just discovering that it might really be worse than I had previously suspected." Howard looked back down at the desk littered with papers and the open ledger, barely making out his company's gaze under the weak lights of the candles overhead and the oil lamp beside him.

Adeline couldn't deny the disappointment she felt at that moment; she'd gone looking for him, and hoping that when she found him, she would simply allow herself fall into his arms, and have him hold her for as long as he could before they felt each other even more. The memories she had dug up earlier were close to souring her mood, and she knew no one better than the man in front of her to get her feeling alive again. But the Howard in whose presence she was now, was the man that exhibited a quite peculiar obsession for facts and answers. The one she had encountered many times in and out of his study and wondered how anyone could be so invested in something the way he often did, as he would stare at the papers that had rows and rows of numbers written in them for hours on end, completely losing himself in them and often deaf and blind to the rest of the world at that time. And sadly, even she wasn't immune to the wall he had around him at such times.

She had really hoped he would not be, for she needed the Howard that had whispered his affection for her into her ears before the break of dawn that morning, but she got her master in his study instead. The help let her gaze — that he made no effort for — drop away as she announced herself again after the moment of silence.

"I see that you're occupied, Master Forsyth, I wanted to inquire if perhaps there was anything you needed before I turned in for the night," she said, keeping the disappointment in her eyes away from him.

Howard tore his own eyes away from the papers in his hold at once, at the unusual courtesy she added to his name. He set the papers on the desk, got up and walked over to the other side to meet his woman.

"Why, Miss Adeline. If I have done something for you to take offence to, I apologize, deeply," he said, as he took her arms she'd crossed in front of her into his, and pulled her closer to himself, so that that her bosom would rest against his unbuttoned chest and their faces would be inches apart.

She looked up at him and couldn't help the smile that took over her face and flattened her prior blueness with a shade of pink that was invisible under the candlelight taking over her cheeks. "You have absolutely nothing to apologize for, Master Howard, I am simply here to offer my services."

"And that, you have every right to do, and yet I apologize for being too carried away, even if the matter is of troubling importance, it should never take precedence over you, my sweet."

She smiled widely, a sight that constantly dazzled Howard. "I don't think I should bother you while you work."

"Nonsense, your company can never be a bother. Besides, I do need a second opinion on these matters. You see, I have been pouring over the details from the ledger I got from Bryce Allen, the accountant who used to work at city hall. He worked with Sir Fitzhugh previously at the mines. I took a look at the documents which I had compiled in the few days that I've worked with the chap, and some things just do not add up. For the mere hour that I have spent at this, I have discovered mysterious figures logged constantly with no particular details, I have discovered that there are these breaks in the quantity of unrefined material exported. The amount logged from the mines suddenly takes a tumble en route to the Forge, and delivery is never questioned. It just disappears with no manner of documentation whatsoever."

"Well where did it go?"

"I don't know. But after comparing this with the account reports Bryce was so reluctant to share with me, it is apparent that things are not as they seem, and this has quite possibly been going on for an extended period of time. I need to get these findings to Lord Palmerston, but I don't know how to get him here."

"What if Fitzhugh finds out that you have discovered these things in his affairs, and he gets wind that you intend to rat him out?"

"I can only assume that It won't be pretty. As a matter of fact, if I do manage to put a letter out to Palmerston myself, Fitzhugh most likely would find out before the letter reaches the messenger's satchel and I might not be here by the time Palmerston gets back. My best chance is to find the most discrete manner in which to convey my thoughts to the Lord himself directly."

"And what best way can you think of, that doesn't involve you traveling to see the Lord in person?"

"Sadly, none at this time. But perhaps there is a way to find out more about the operations, right underneath Fitzhugh's nose, as it is his very own idea even; he has requested me to help with one of the trains, perhaps if I joined it, I could be able to tell where all the missing materials go to."

"What if I was able to help with reaching out to him?"

"Fitzhugh?"

"No. Lord Palmerston."

"And how exactly would you manage that? As much as it maddens, we both know that no one would pay much mind to sending a letter for you, much less one to Palmerston. It is the way things are, unjust."

Adeline took no offence at his words; she knew he was right and that reminding her was not in any way about him telling her of her place. She knew Howard was no such man, she knew he simply had no clue as to how she could really manage it. And she smiled at his innocent ignorance; the man was yet to know half of what the real Adeline was about. "Sir Dayton, one of the county's councilmen, and the Queen's royal counsel. I watch his last born, Tom, most days and every evening, I have some, though restricted, level of access to his household, I could find a way to make it seem as if he is the one sending Lord Palmerston the word."

Howard had his eyes widened in surprise.

"How about you just bother yourself with simply writing that letter, in Sir Dayton's address and getting it to me. I'll get it sent across to him, in the meantime, what will you be doing?" She asked with the half the smile still hidden on her face.

"Ensuring nothing goes missing tomorrow. And if it does, I will be relaying the information to Palmerston when he arrives. Are you absolutely certain you can manage this, Adeline? I don't want to burden you with a task so—"

"Howard."

"I know, I know, but if something were to happen to you. I wouldn't, I could never forgive myself."

"You should. While I would be, in part, doing it for the man I love..." Adeline caught her breath as she realized she had never said it out loud, its sound, incredibly foreign to her. "...I will also be doing this because maybe someday, what I do will change the way women and those of the lowest class are perceived, and we will be allowed the same rights and freedoms as normal human beings if not everyone else."

Howard stared at her; his mouth slightly agape. She giggled at the look on his face, before pushing herself away from him.

"Maybe you should be queen."

Adeline laughed, her hand quickly covering her mouth as it was a tad too high pitched and it was night time. "Maybe I should."

"And I would give all that I have, including my life, just to see that day."

Adeline's smile suddenly became heavier on her face as her heart thudded at the words about him losing his life for her, she felt a sudden call of déjà vu; her mother's story. And it hit her in the pit of her stomach, something Howard was yet to know. And his face unclear under the low lights suddenly troubled her for no reason. She'd wanted to very much to be in his arms at the moment, but she knew still that Howard, the auditor needed the night to himself.

"I know you would, Howard, and I hope you never have to."

This time, he was the one smiling, "I'll have the letter ready for you by morning before they arrive to pick me up. Please take great care, Adeline."

"I will, Howard. Good night."

He watched her leave, and a small part of his heart went cold. Howard loved this woman and he knew it, with every passing day, he would get reaffirmed of the fact. He resented parting from her presence, or being unable to reach her for extended periods. The thought of coming home and seeing her brought a warmth to his body that nothing else could. He admired her resolve and drive to change the status quo, something he was interested in doing as well, mainly because he wanted to be with her.

That was his drive. That was why he kept the candles burning all night, tallying the records from the documents in the ledger and producing an itemized list of shortages in a chronological order. He found wage bills that constantly failed to tally with the registered workers at the mines, and though that might have been associated with the uncertainty of the events as he'd witnessed first-hand, the discrepancies still were bothersome. But his most important discovery were the requests papers which had been forged with an entire shipment of steel gone. Howard couldn't help but wonder what uses Fitzhugh had found for it, perhaps he sold it on the black market or to enemy forces. Whatever it was, the Queen would have his head.

FIVE

A fter gathering his findings late into the night and the early hours of the following morning, he wrote the letter for Palmerston, inviting him to the Dayton's annual ball and the wedding ceremony of his Niece, Parthenia.

Howard tried to get a few minutes of rest, but dawn would be upon them before his body has a befitting rest. And before his eyes could find the kind of sleep that would forget the work they had done the hours before, Archie and his cart would probably already be waiting outside the house.

He quickly had his breakfast as it was already being prepared by Adeline by the time he woke. No one else seemed to be awake at the time, as they rattled about the large house, just the two of them, giving Howard a feel of what it would be like, to live unbothered with the woman of his heart. He would do anything to make that dream a reality and he intended to.

Archie took him to the mine without as much as a single word. The air between them seemed stifled with tension, something Howard did his best to avoid. He had arrived at his office without Edmund today. He had chosen to go without him as a precautionary measure — less things to worry about if he wasn't around. Howard waited till late afternoon, after the returns of the morning shipment had gone out. Once the train returned, Howard took off to find Fitzhugh, suggesting to follow the train.

Fitzhugh obliged without a second thought, showing him to the train once it was fully loaded with its maximum output. It was different from the other conventional carrier trains as it had only two coaches. One for the individuals aboard it and the second for the engine room. It had four large buckets in which the large casts of partly refined steel were held, ready for transport. A worker from the mine explained the workings of the locomotive to Howard, as they were shorthanded due to the cave in.

He would be the only one on the train. The steam-powered vehicle ran nearly entirely on its own, as all Howard had to do was regulate the coals heating up the engine and refill the steam tank with water when it fell short. He would do it about four times in the total time it would take him to get from the mine to the docks. For a man that couldn't remember the last time he drew his own bath, Howard had to roll up his sleeves and shuttle the water for the train from the stream back and forth until it was fully loaded. He took the document for the shipment that had been prepared, adding it to his ledger. Once on board the train, he poured over it, double checking the load with the numbers written in the document. It was simple and straightforward, and at the end, he realized that the entire shipment was actually complete without any hint of mischievousness. Fitzhugh had let him see what he wanted, but it was far from being that easy.

The train ran along the edge of the coast, miles away from the city, but just close enough to the beach for its rail lines to be laid. Howard appreciated being alone on the train, it gave him a chance to appreciate the beauty of the countryside. The spring trees had turned on their deep vibrant greenness and flowers in full bloom peppered the plains and a few valleys, a contrast that was admired by few. He could smell the sea breeze from there, enjoying the moment.

A bell that notified the coachman whenever the water had run short gave a little ring, its second one since the journey had begun. He was about halfway from the docks and in the middle of the wilderness. He grabbed the bucket and went at it, carrying the water from its reserve tank behind the coaches on the far end of the train where the steel was being stored. As he filled the buckets, he saw a small mound of a black substance heaped in a corner.

Howard placed the bucket down and pinched the substance which he suspected was coal between his fingers, sniffing it. The substance appeared to be sulfur, a peculiar smell he was familiar with as it was the main substance used in the pistol he had brought with him. He had cleaned it out and loaded it with pellets and a generous amount of gunpowder before Archie arrived.

Seeing the gunpowder on the floor, his mind flashed back to the coach where he had done his work from. He remembered seeing something similar running around the edge of the coach, but he dismissed it as he worked, completely ignorant of what it was.

Realization struck the man, causing him to dash into the coach, grabbing his briefcase. As he quickly packed up his documents, his eyes strayed to the gunpowder where it lined the floors of the chamber, confirming the fact that the train had been rigged for an explosion, and fear gripped at his heart. The auditor exited the coach as quickly as he could and made his way into the ones at the back that stored the steel, and as soon as he stepped there, he noticed a cloud of dust moving alongside the train. When he looked closer her saw what the dust had been trailing; two steam carts, running after the locomotive. He spotted one of its occupants lift something that looked like a crossbow which had a burning arrow at its tip, before Howard could react, the arrow left the bow and landed on the rigged coach.

The explosion rocked the train, causing the behemoth of a machine to swerve to the left dangerously, almost derailing the it. The coach had been completely destroyed, leaving only its base. Howard emerged from where he had crouched at the birth of the blast, wielding his briefcase as a shield, he took the said container and shoved it between two large steel beams, and pulled out his only weapon from underneath his jacket, uncertain how he was going to manage with it alone. The cart was right beside him, separated from where he was by the walls of the train. He looked through the space in between the wooden boards of the train to see the two vehicles racing behind the him. Five men, three of them armed. One of them was dressed in a contraption that looked incredibly foreign to him.

Howard watched in terror as the man in the car leaped up, spreading his arms. He gawked as lightweight steel beams extended along the arms of the man, along with a length of silk material dropping underneath it. There was a light humming sound coming from the contraption, one which Howard recognized as a steam engine. Somehow, they had successfully miniaturized one into something as small as a backpack. It allowed the man to drift through the air, gaining on the train quickly. Howard knew that if they found him first, it would certainly spell his end. He summoned all the courage he could muster and rushed out with his pistol out in front. The auditor had only ever fired at small game animals, back when he and his father used to go hunting; he had never been at odds with another man enough to be in the position where he had to point a gun at him let alone shoot, but now fazed with enemies that numbered the fingers of his hand, who did not seem to be keen on talking through their differences, he knew he had only a handful of shots, and if he did not make each one of them count, he would become history very quickly.

The first steamcart gained on the train even more, and the man in the passenger's side jumped off and caught onto the back coach. Howard put his head out by the side, peeked at the man before aligning his right arm as well as he could, recalling the pointers his old man had given him, and firing. The bullet hit the man right beneath his raised arm, causing him to lose his grip and fall off the train. His head bounced off the metal of the rails before his body rolled to a stop. Shots rang off the cart as the other men fired back, their bullets meeting Howard's cover that was the wooden wall of the coach and ricocheting. One bullet however hit the wood closely enough, splinting it and sending its fragments into Howard's uncovered forearm.

He swore, gripping at the fresh tears on his skin, with the surrounding areas quickly turning a pale pink. He quickly retreated further into the coach, out of sight of the men in the cart. Once inside, his attention left his pierced arm as he heard a thump on the roof of the coach, with the man in the flying contraption making use of his machine. Howard froze, listening for the man's steps, only to hear the ear-splitting sound of a blunderbuss. The gun was fired inside from the roof, creating a large gape in it, with the pellets hitting the floor next Howard.

Howard spun on the balls of his feet running forwards, back into the coach that had been blown apart. He peeked out over the scorched doorway to see the boot of the man. It connected with his face, throwing

Howard to the floor. Howard looked up through a blurred vision to see the man quickly trying to reload the weapon. Unwilling to find out what that would mean, Howard fired his pistol at him, missing the shot wildly, but with enough grease to make the man wary. He retreated, brandishing the weapon as he shoved the pellets down its barrel and pushed it down.

An idea occurred to the auditor as he watched the man on the roof. He took off running towards the engine room where the water tank had been dried up, once the compression chambers lost its steam, the engine would die out. Howard knew this, but he came for something else. As the man with the steam-powered wings aimed his gun at Howard, waiting for him to hold still so he would blow the auditor to kingdom come, he felt a sudden force throw him forward as his target pulled on a large steel lever attached to the floor of the engine room. As Howard cut the brakes, the man fell forwards, over the coach and off the train to the ground beside it.

It was accompanied by a loud bang as the man's body got rammed into by one of the carts, destroying it. The rider was thrown out face-first into the dirt. Howard pulled the lever back, unclamping the brakes as the engines coughed and sputtered, accelerating but just barely. The second steam cart was catching up and the engines would die out soon. Howard rushed back to the last coach, hefting two buckets this time dumping the load of the first one into the engine. He turned to see one of the three men in the cart leap onto the last coach.

He watched as the second man timed his jump, looking for the right moment to make his move. As he leaped, Howard threw the second bucket of water in his direction. Majority of it missed him and the bucket was knocked aside by the cart and the water did little to deter him. Howard climbed to the top of the locomotive, looking through the hole blown open by the previous assailant, he fired two shots which hit its target, killing one of the men instantly.

The second one returned his shots through the roof, with the bullets missing Howard by mere inches. He returned three shots of his own, firing blindly with the hopes of hitting him. Howard heard the man run out behind him, so he threw himself flat against the roof so his enemy would not get a good angle on the shot he was desperate for. His attacker jumped up in the air and fired at the roof, his bullet flying through the air as Howard was nowhere in sight. Confused, the man looked to the left side of the train, to see his colleague in the cart making gestures to him. As he turned to the other side, he got tackled into the coach.

Howard jammed his gun against the man's neck, trying to incapacitate his opponent. The man was physically stronger than him; he could easily shove Howard off the locomotive. He lifted his pistol to fire but then Howard had had to be quick thinking all through the ride with every cell in his body trying to ignore the fear, doing all he could to avoid death, he knocked the gun out of the man's hands, a bit surprised he was successful. The man lifted his hands up to the side of his face, readying for a fist fight. Howard knew he wouldn't last against a man of his size in hand-to-hand combat, so he swung his now-empty pistol on its butt which was made of pure steel and connected the hilt with the side of the man's head with as much force as he could manage. The large man went down like a rock, knocked out instantly.

Only the man in the steamcart remained, driving beside them as the train chugged forward through the countryside. Howard hauled and threw the body of his comrade out the side of the train into his path, but he dodged it quickly, learning from the mistakes of the previous vehicle. He went behind the train, ready to evade any other attempt by Howard. But he hadn't prepared for one thing, Howard cut the straps that held the steel beams in place and pushed them to the side, it hit the wooden walls, breaking it to planks and that scattered out behind the train.

One of the beams hit the cart, impaling its driver. Howard watched, shocked and relieved at the same time as the wreckage shrunk in size behind him, with the train unbothered by the events as it continued speeding off to the docks with half its load out by the tracks. He picked up the gun he had knocked out of the hands of one of the men and inspected it. He counted six rounds inside the pistol, they were not nearly enough to breed confidence, but he was quite low on choice, he would have to make do. He rested his back against the side of the coach for the first time in nearly half an hour, realizing he had almost really lost his life, and he had somehow survived. The ache of his injuries was birthed, but he was yet to arrive at his destination. He did not know what he would find at the docks, he had no idea what Fitzhugh would have prepared for him there too, but he was not going to stop. The auditor checked his briefcase to see it was still there, and the ledger had been untroubled throughout the fiasco. He turned and simply hung on as the steam machine continued to take him to his next challenge.

Sir Dayton and his household held the tradition of inviting folks of the highest of class like themselves to a gathering once every year, a tradition that was started by his mother who was best friends with the Queen's mother when they were alive. Their annual event was like tens of others by other families, that took turns to host their chums form different parts of the county. Sir Archibald Dayton was perhaps the second in authority among the Queen's councilmen, only behind none other than the Lord Palmerston himself who was in charge of all the steel mining activities for the queen. Sir Dayton's opinion was highly valued by the council and the queen as held the office that was responsible for trade negotiations with other colonies. Officially, he was the county's foreign ambassador on matters that had to do with trade, and the man he would need be inviting to the ball that would coincide with his niece's wedding was a friend of his.

In Sir Dayton's mansion, there were more rooms than Adeline could probably ever be certain of. As she'd told Howard, she was but a visiting help, whose presence only ever mattered about the wellness of the household's last child and heir to his father's affluence and status. Wherever she stepped needed to be in regard of the child or his needs, however little. Left to say she was not allowed to wonder aimlessly let alone lose her way or pause in front of the Master's study chamber. And her mere presence inside without an undefeatable reason could quite possibly mean her end, and not just as the child's help but as a person with life, the commoner that she was.

The upper elite had their secrets and affairs that never left their circles, the lords and masters conducted the direst of businesses in their studies, where they could sometimes leave behind evidence of the events, which meant the chambers were considered sacred, perhaps the most important room in the entire house even. And Sir Dayton was no ordinary man. He knew things only those closest to the Queen's circle were aware of. Adeline would be risking everything to get in that room, she knew this, but Samantha's daughter that was friends with Thomas and Oswald who had done the wildest of things to survive when they were kids was no stranger to risks.

The Daytons' butler, two other helps, a house guard and the mutt named Lam were the only ones in the house with Tom and Adeline, Mrs. Dayton was out for Tuesday brunch with her friends before the wall clock sounded for midday. Adeline had watched her carriage trot off herself from the window of the child's room, making certain that the lady disappeared far into the distance before she began to ponder again on her steps. She had just two things to worry about; the butler that could come and check up on the child anytime on her mother's order, and the mutt that hardly stayed in one place for too long. The mutt, she had prepared for though; she'd brought a piece of leftover chicken dumb-bell from Howard's breakfast with her, and it was certain to keep the loud pet busy at least till she was done with her mission, hence really, her main problem was the ever-watchful butler, Julius.

The chief manservant of the house wasn't so particular about Adeline or her seldom presence in the house, no more than the other servants that were around, and she had never had the cause to be in his way, but his duties could very much be the bane of her task that afternoon. She waited a while, studying for the positions that everyone else had taken at their duties. The guard was almost never inside the house, the other helps had been buried in the kitchen preparing for Sir Dayton's dinner later that evening. But Julius still had no particular post, he went almost wherever he pleased, he was like the house's very own warden, keeping an eye on the helps in the absence of the owners.

Adeline talked Tom into taking a stroll downstairs to the garden and the kid obliged on the condition that she would tell him another of her stories by the time she would tuck him in come bedtime. She might not have been able to allow herself admit it, but a part of her was slowly feeling the boy's connection to her with each night she spent being the last face he saw before he fell asleep.

From the moment they were out of the boy's room, she had begun to scope her targets, the study, which was located on the other side of the building. She could not make out the entrance until she was either down the stairs or coming back up again. Her other target by the way, moved just past them as she and the kid headed to the back garden. Adeline avoided any eye contact with the man, pretending to be totally invested in her duties which was none other than the boy whose hand was in hers. The kid too was more than pleased to be spending time with someone who really cared about little things he loved to do, he looked up at her feigned glance and showed his wide smile with the gaps in his missing teeth stealing the show. And yet Adeline's heart was warmed.

They made it to the garden without Adeline looking back, unsure if the butler had taken any suspicion to their walk, and unwilling to foster his thoughts should their gazes meet. Tom did not release her hand as he ran towards the swing that was suspending with chains from the very thick branch of tree that took a fair portion of the field, causing Adeline to hurry with him unconsciously, and drawing her out of her worry about the butler for a moment. They arrived at the swing and Tom instantly got himself in the seat.

"Come on Adeline, push, push!" He said, and the help obliged, positioning herself behind him with a smile on her face. She placed her hands around the seat and nudged the little lord forward, forcing a loud yell of excitement from him as he propelled into the air. They continued this as Adeline enjoyed her company with the kid, just as she kept her eye on the building, hoping for the time when the butler would step out and she could have a better window. He might have been a critical servant, but one thing Adeline also knew was that he couldn't do without smoking.

Almost every other hour, she knew he would have to at some point in time step outside for a smoke. The butler did his business outside because Mrs. Dayton detested the smell of burning tobacco in the house. She only ever endured it whenever her husband or his posh company smoked, and once they started, she would find a way to excuse herself. So, Julius knew better than to leave the house reeking of it till the lady of the house returned.

She had almost begun to doubt if he would really show, as her palms had started to come a little sore for the swing she was pushing, and just before she could start to think about another way to do what she needed with the butler lurking, the man stepped out, glanced at her and Tom and headed to the other side of the building, his preferred spot, that allowed him a view while he turned the light on his cigarette and scarred his lungs away. And once he was out of their sight, Adeline let go of Tom and quickly asked the kid to continue playing while she took care of a little business inside, and Tom was more than cooperative with his nanny.

It was public knowledge that Sir Dayton and Lord Palmerston were acquaintances, it was a fairly public knowledge that Archibald wrote to him almost every other week regarding the interests of both their official and social capacities. But Adeline had been the one to overhear him tell his wife that he would have to wait till after the dinner to send his letters for the week, seeing how his messenger has abruptly caught a flu. That meant that she knew he would still have Palmerston's letter somewhere in his study, and all she had to do was find it and replace it with the one Howard had written, and she had to do that quickly in the window it would take the butler to finish his smoke.

She ran up the stairs and right of the house this time, instead of the usual left where Tom's room was, she passed one door which she was yet to figure what was behind it, and reached the other that would open to her target. The scanned her sides for peering eyes as she turned the knob on the door, finding it unlocked, and she stepped in and gently closed the door behind herself.

The room was larger than she imagined, almost twice the size of Howard's, and it wall better furnished too, but she had no time to admire the furniture, so she got to work at the large desk and started looking around for where Sir Dayton might have kept the letters he intended to send. She did not have to work so hard, as they sat on top of each other on the other side of the desk with would have been the writer's left since the Lord was naturally left-handed. She found four of them in total, and quickly sort on their addresses for Palmerston's name, and she found it. She dug the replacement out from inside her brassiere and put it in the stack, then took Dayton's letter to replace its successor. Adeline adjusted her dress, and prepared for her final task; a clean exit.

"The most important rule when sneaking into anywhere is to never look out of place." Thomas's words played in her head as she turned the knob on the door and stepped out of the study, turning around to do the opposite as silently as she could. Immediately, she had her hands on the side of her dress like she were adjusting it just as she began her journey for the stairs, and butler Julius emerged, standing right in front of her, with the pair hardly a foot apart so that she was able to inhale the scent of burnt tobacco that still swam around him.

"What business of yours do you have in this part of the building?!" He stormed at her and she froze for just a second at the terror in his tone, even though he was nothing but a glorified servant, Adeline knew he could still make things very unpleasing for her. She could not avoid to keep the eye contact with him, because it would simply reassure the man that she had something to hide. She stood her ground, and dusted well on her dress.

"I needed to take care of business in the loo, and the one here was the closest I could reach. Have I done something wrong in that regard?" She said, wiping on her dress even firmer to allow the man's mind dwell in the trick; the absurdity of him asking a lady what she was doing in restroom.

The butler looked flushed, like he wanted to say something but her subtle gestures really did work, as his eyes left her gaze for further down her dress, he closed his mouth and ground his jaw just as Tom sounded for his buddy from the back of the house.

"Adeline…" the child called.

"Yes Tom, I'm here!" She answered, not leaving the front of the butler yet, "would you like me to show you what I did in there, or can I return to caring for the little sir?" She said, not missing a beat in her stance or her gaze at him, even though her heart was beating crazily, ready to burst out of her chest. But she had him already, she made him uncomfortable, the master's child, his master, needed and called for her, and Adeline barely broke a sweat.

"Keep to the side of the building you're allowed, and mind nothing but the little sir. That, is your business." He said before he stepped aside to let her pass.

Adeline nodded, brushing the man's ego just enough to get him off her back, and she returned down the stairs and back to the garden where her business was waiting.

She did not know for certain; she had simply taken the wildest of gambles and it worked; she had studied the entire house more and more as she arrived to care for Tom, and she had put the pieces of the large house together in her mind. The wing where Tom's room was had one other room; a seemingly vacant one and a convenience she often used when she visited, Tom's room had its own convenience attached too, so it simply made sense if there was a spare one in the other wing of the house if the master's bedroom already had its.

Adeline walked towards the little sir where he'd sat devoid of cheer in her absence, and she called at him, "I'm here now, shall we continue?" She said, and the child's face grew back the smile he'd lost at once.

Looking at him react to seeing her that way made it hard for Adeline to see Tom as nothing more than the innocent child who wanted the little things that brought happiness to him. His small mind was yet to be poisoned with hatred for people like her; people of her class and status, who the Queen had declared unworthy of living a proper life. He was yet to begin the stage of his life where he would have to look down on the girls of the southern colonies, and have nothing but disgust for their appearance so he can look normal to his chums of equally elite status as himself, even if he thought the one girl in the middle with the red hair looked amazing. Right then, Tom was just a child, privileged, but a child nonetheless and she hoped that the things she would be able to do would mean he would not grow to being the classist jerk the Queen wanted.

SIX

H oward got a horse from a man by the docks. By evening, he was back in town, where he secured his briefcase before continuing for the mines with the pistol in tow. Fitzhugh had tried to kill him and get rid of the information regarding his criminal activities, and he had survived. A part of him told him it would be nothing short of being incredibly stupid to go back into the lion's den, but he knew Fitz would not physically assault him, not in front of so many workers, or at least he hoped he wouldn't.

He received stares from everyone who watched him as he rode in, a sleeve of his shirt had been bloodied up, and black sooth from the explosion painted the once white material a deep gray.

"Fitzhugh!" His voice carried through the mines, echoing as everyone stopped to watch. He got off the horse and realized what a dumb move he had made. There was no way he would be able to see Fitzhugh if he was down in the mines.

"Howard."

He whipped out the pistol as he turned around at the sound of Fitzhugh's voice, but an arm went around his, nearly twisting fully across it. It locked in with the small of his elbow, pulling him into a half Nelson which he inverted by lifting Howard and slamming him into the ground. He looked up to see Archie whip the gun away and drive his knee into his temple. Howard struggled, but Archie pushed the knee further into the side of his face, reaffirming his desire — stay down.

"You tried to have me killed you bastard!"

With a wave, Archie got off his face and took a long step to stand beside Fitzhugh. His face looked almost apologetic but his actions stated otherwise. He picked up the gun and folded it into his waistband.

"I don't know what you're talking about."

Howard's eyes went wide as he panted to regain his breath from the manner he had been disarmed, Archie standing next to Fitzhugh was the one thing keeping him from trying to tackle the man. The adrenaline from nearly dying on the train was very much still coursing through his bloodstream, and hence the auditor was feeling fairly invincible. "Your men attacked me. Five of them, in steamcarts, they were armed, with certainly no intentions of ensuring my safety to the docks."

"I'm afraid you must have mistaken; my men did no such type of thing."

"So how would you explain all of this? I nearly died, Fitzhugh. You even went as far as rigging the train, hoping it would explode with me in it?"

"Howard, of what delusions do you speak? I have no idea what you came across on your trip to the docks, as I certainly did not try kill you. Going to the docks was simply a favor for the mine being short of men, and I assumed you could also get to see for yourself the end of the entire process from the mines, which is the delivery. You seemed quite curious."

"Oh, enough with the horse crap, Fitzhugh! I know what you are up to! Let me tell you, I'm on to you, and it won't be long at all. Just you wait."

Fitzhugh walked over to him amidst all the stares. The mines had been cleared out for the day, only a few slackers or people who were looking to work overtime remained. Still it was more than enough for Howard to base his speculations of his safety, he swallowed a lump of saliva as the man got closer. When the former soldier was within earshot, he spoke in a hushed whisper.

"You know I could make certain you're gone before dawn. The only reason you're here now is because I permit it, and that, I do for a reason. I don't really want to kill you, Howard, you're an intelligent man who would prove to be a valuable asset to me when the time comes. But you need to stop making a nuisance of yourself, you need to put an end to whatever tricks you might think you have up your bloody sleeves. Prove to me that your alliances are nothing against my affairs. Get out of my way, Forsyth, and you can have everything you desire."

Howard let what he had heard play over in his head, Fitzhugh stretched out an open palm, offering it to him. A sign of acceptance and allegiance, a quick solution. The auditor leaned forward and spat on the floor next to Fitzhugh. "To hell with allegiance with you. I know what becomes of men who get in bed with the likes of you. You're a monster, a man who ruins lives at will. And what I desire cannot be bought with all of the riches in Greene County. You'll never have me, Fitzhugh, never!"

"Are you sure about that?" Fitzhugh responded under his breath, before turning away from him. "You might want to go into town first."

The man walked away, heading for a cave behind him as the small crowd that had gathered behind them parted for him to pass. Archie still stood between them, hand on the pistol. In one swift motion, he emptied the weapon of its projectiles before tossing both at Howard. He walked towards the auditor, bumping shoulders with him aggressively as he walked past. Howard caught a bit of what he had mumbled under his breath as he left.

The crowd had begun to thin and Howard too had begun to feel he needed some rest; wearing off, the rush of adrenaline that had saw him survive the day was also bound to leave him spent. His arm ached the most from where the splinters had cut him, they needed to be looked at, as he had left the wound open for quite some time. His father's warnings mentally reprimanded him as he remembered the instructions that were given to him when he was younger about open wounds and infections.

He decided he would grab the briefcase later, hopefully as soon as he was certain that the letter had been sent out and Lord Palmerston was on its way. Howard knew if anyone could stop Fitzhugh, it was him.

As he rode home on the horse, a thought occurred to him that hadn't taken priority at the time he was trying not to get killed: The men who had attacked him on the train, while he didn't recognize them at once, looked somewhat familiar. He had seen a couple of them at the mines a number of times, where they worked quite closely with Fitzhugh himself. And yet the bastard still denied sending men after him. The one who had worn the flying contraption gnawed at Howard.

He could not stop wondering where Fitzhugh had gotten such a machine from. He wondered how the things had been possible. It obviously was no simple feat of engineering, but for it to be attached to a random man who was sent to kill him, certainly there was more. Fitzhugh had claimed he and his men built the monstrous one he'd watched them use the other day at the mine, but Howard had his doubts about it from the very moment the words had left his mouth. Besides, making machines like that was certain to cost its fair amount of money and resources, even the steam carts. They weren't that rampant yet, although some states had their versions of the vehicle, the last week or so had been the first time that Howard had seen and ridden anything like that. Then it struck.

The undefined figures that had been part of his discovery in the ledger from Bryce Allen, the one that seemingly had no trail to be followed. The numbers were sales. The steel. Fitzhugh had been stealing and selling the steel and using it to make his steam-powered contraptions. But something else was missing. Why was he making it? Perhaps for commercial sale? But if that were the case, then every elite in town would have their own private steamcart instead of a carriage. It wasn't for commercial sale, none of the items seemed to be put out there to the public. Whatever reason Fitzhugh was making these things were incomprehensible to Howard.

He stopped down the street from his house to see three men waiting out in front. Their long-belted overcoats, batons, and unique hats signaled to Howard that they were of the royal guard. He wondered why they were at his home so late, standing outside. One of them turned around and spotted him, his eyes went wide with realization and recognition.

"There he is! Get him!" the guard screamed and took off running after him, the other two in tow. Howard pulled the reigns on the horse, making a U-turn heading back in the direction he had come. The horse plowed down the cobbled floors of the streets, making it easy for them men to follow him with the sound of the hooves trotting the paved floor. They were no match for the horse as it quickly left them behind, entering a path through the trees in the side of the road. A shortcut that would lead to the part of town the elite never wanted to hear of.

Howard stopped the horse, alighted and smacked it on its rear, sending the animal running off in the opposite direction from where he was going. It was cold out there as the night sky had come in full effect, the moon shone brightly through the thick canopy of trees which Howard ran through, occasionally obscured by a cloud or two. The sound of the night forest filled his ear, but he knew exactly where he was headed so he kept running as quickly as his legs could manage, he was really beginning to tire; never in his lifetime had Howard Forsyth been through the amount of trouble he'd been, not in a single day. It was as if he were another man entirely, not the sophisticated, middle-class, paper-watching auditor that he was. The entire day had birthed a side of him he had no idea existed. And it sure was getting overwhelming.

The forest vanished into a small clearing, where beyond it were a spree of wooden houses. He slowed his run into a quick-paced casual walk, trying not to draw attention from the locals that lurked outside that evening. The further he got, the more he wondered what it was that the queen had against the people that lived there. He had seldom been to that part of town, it was dangerous for men like him to be there without any type of protection, regardless of his intentions. The hostility the people had received from those regarded as the better class, they tended to repay whenever they got the chance, and a man such as himself, who though held no bitterness towards them could really see the ugly side of the colonies if he was made, just for the way he was dressed. He did have the pistol with him, but there was no way he was going to draw any attention to himself or where he was headed.

It was the biggest house in the area by both size and structure, compared to the state the rest were too, it stood better. It was the only one that had a proper second floor and perhaps the only one that actually had a working chimney. And the bricks which held the house together for whatever warm and vibrant look it had before now, looked old and grimy under the monochrome dimness of the night light. The broad oak tree that sat next to the building like an extra wall that had gained its own life, gave it an ominous look in the dark night, with its sprawled branches shielding the better part of the house from whatever light the night shone.

Howard ran up the short stairs that led up to the front porch, each one of them creaking under his weight. The house certainly had seen better days but still looked kept. He knocked loudly thrice on the hardwood door, and it was answered almost immediately. A slide opened from behind the door, giving way to a pair of eyes illuminated by a candle that stared through the space in the door. A deep female voice came from the other end.

"And who might you to be?"

"I'm Howard, I'm here to—"

"Howard who?"

"Howard Forsyth. Is A—"

"Yes, of course, and I be Queen Victoria."

"Look! I need to find Adeline, is she home?"

There was a pause and the sound of feet leaving the door. Howard saw his breath form in front of him. He waited for a second, hoping that the lady who had answered had gone to get a key or something. Fear tugged at him, causing him to knock again right as the door was thrown open by Adeline. She pulled him into a hug first, before closing the door and turning the deadbolt and crossbeam.

"Howard, thank heavens you're safe! What's going on? The guards are after you. They claim there's been a murder and you're the suspect."

"What? Murder? Of whom? I was being chased by them. I did not know why, and I could not think of anywhere else to turn which they wouldn't search. Whose murder are they accusing me of?"

"The old accountant."

"Bryce Allen? He's dead? How did that happen? I... Have you heard from Edmund?"

"Not for a while, no. What happened at the mines, why do you look so disheveled? What happened to your arm?" she said, noticing the starched blood that patterned his dressing and peering at it.

"Who is this?" Came an old croaky voice from behind Adeline.

Howard turned to see an older lady walking towards him, cane in hand as she balanced herself out. She walked with a slight limp, angling herself towards the light so she could get a good look at Howard. She squinted at him, snorting loudly as though displeased by who she saw. She looked from his torn shirt to bloodied arm with disdain and disapproval, shaking her head.

"Ma Saleh, this is the man I..."

"I know who he is." She interrupted with a voice louder than Howard could have predicted. "Strong jawline, eyes like those, that voice and posture. You're a Forsyth, are you not?"

"Yes, Madam. Howard Forsyth. I wouldn't have c —
"

"I don't want to hear it. You're the one who has been working my girl to the bone aren't you? That sniveling jackanape of a man called Edmund lied to me and placed her in your household, and you chip away at Adeline as though she is some machine built for you."

"Ma Sa…"

"Shush, girl. Forsyth, that girl in you see, is my daughter, and I will not have her in harm's way, not for any reason, and certainly not for a man who comes from a feeble blood like yours. Unless you're willing to risk everything, I will no longer have her working for you. What do you have to say for yourself?"

Howard stared at the older woman as he suddenly became aware of what he had been asked. "If you will allow me, Ma'am, I love Adeline you see, with all of my heart, and I would do every single thing that I can to make certain I get to spend the rest of my life with her. Indeed, Madam, I'm prepared to give up everything for your girl." he said, ending the words at Adeline's gaze.

A sharp knock suddenly hit the door and stripped the union of the moment, followed by the sound of the guards announcing themselves. Madam Saleh smiled at Howard, before motioning to Adeline to take him upstairs. She went over to the door, calling the girl who had responded to Howard at first to open it up. The men looked about to jump inside before they recognized the old lady.

"Is there a problem?"

"Evening, Madam Saleh. Not at all, it's just that there's been a murder and we have been trying to track down the man who is responsible. You wouldn't happen to have run into a man by the name of Howard Forsyth anytime recent, have you? He's the town auditor."

"Forsyth? Yes. The name does ring a bell. Why, I knew his father. You know, he and I, we used to be very good friends back in the day, back when I was still young and beautiful, and he hadn't become the town physician that wanted to treat only the elite." Saleh coughed and stumbled forwards, causing a guard to reach out, catching her and holding her upright. "Thank you, so much."

The guard was young, naïve and really cautious of the old lady, "Just doing my duty. Perhaps we can take a look around?"

"To what end? All you'll find are my girls. Why would a high city man like Forsyth be here?"

"Still, we have to make sure. Sorry for the inconvenience, Madam Saleh."

The guard helped her to a chair while the others went on into the labyrinth of the house, peeking through door after door. Howard hid right behind the door of the room that Adeline had come to call her own. They heard the man's boots coming up the stairs, causing her to act fast. Adeline pulled off her gown and wrapped her body in a shawl, revealing a fair portion of her back and shoulders, turning away from the door.

As the guard opened the door, the lady screamed, pretending to be dressing up, pulling the shawl higher up. He mumbled a quick apology and left the room, poked up to the bone. They regrouped at the ground floor, apologizing to Saleh before they left the building.

Howard waited a full ten minutes before he came back out to the kitchen where Adeline had some splint, spirit and tweezers to help clean up the injury on his arm.

"And where is the ledger now?"

"I have kept it hidden away. I don't want to have it on me in case Fitzhugh makes an attempt on my life again," Adeline's eyes locked on his as he said the words, and she paused for a second and took it in. "Or I get arrested," the man continued, "If I'm separated from it for too long without keeping an eye on it, it might just be the end of all our efforts."

"Word is you killed Bryce Allen." Saleh spoke from the back as she returned to the house. The older woman was a lot more agile than she let on. "I'm sure that is not true."

"It is not."

"Good. Then we need to clear your name. Who else was present the last time you saw Bryce?"

"He had a manservant. He locked up after I had left, he would know for sure that I wasn't the one." He flinched as the spirit stung the injury. Adeline rubbed his wrist lightly, holding his palm.

"Then we need to find this servant. He will clear your name and all will be fine. So, what is this about a ledger?" Saleh asked as she settled into an armchair in a way that reminded Howard of a hen settling down into its nest.

"I obtained a ledger from Bryce Allen just a few nights ago that contains details of transactions of the mines under the watch of Sir Fitzhugh White. Lord Palmerston requested I help in monitoring the financial affairs of the facility, since the old accountant's indisposition, and as it turns out, there are a lot of things that are not as they should be, and a lot that are not what they really appear too. The evidence of these things that Sir Fitzhugh has permitted and in fact is responsible for are buried deep within the ledgers. Records that have had to be kept as regards the mines being a property of Greene County and the Queen."

"And I'm guessing Fitzhugh is not that keen on you telling all of this to the Lord Palmerston?"

"No, he certainly isn't. He's made that clear more times than I would like to remember, today alone. And

I'm afraid he will not quit until he knows I will be eternally silent on the matter, whatever that may require." The man said, turning to Adeline whose hold on his arm had turned almost to a grip. Like she was scared for the things he was saying.

"It appears so. So, do you think Allen's murder is still Fitzhugh trying to get you quiet, or is it possible that is something else?"

"I think Fitzhugh is a man that is capable of doing anything to get what he wants. Even if that includes murdering another man, a former acquaintance of his for that matter, and pinning it on me."

"I wouldn't put it past him either. I've lived long enough to know what men in this county one does not deal with, and Fitzhugh tops that list on any given day." Saleh said, looking away at burning lamp a yard from her reach, like she was trying to whisk away the memories.

"I think I can find Bryce's servant. Perhaps I could convince him to talk to you and help declare you innocent." Adeline added.

"I don't think you should, Adeline. After what I experienced today, I really think we should take better caution. This could be dangerous. If Bryce truly was murdered, the murderer could still be out there watching. I'm not going to let you put yourself at risk like that."

"Howard, you can't go out to do anything yourself. Not at the moment. If you're caught, the guards could even have you dead by morning before you get any chance at a trial. We need you to stay until Lord Palmerston gets here." Adeline begged.

"She's right, Forsyth. You do well to listen to her. Now, she might be a lady, and my own girl, but she is a thousand times tougher than she looks. Let her help you. Stay as long as you have to. Your father used to love it here anyway." Saleh said.

SEVEN

H e might have been a true hustler that ran himself out of the south to become a cigar smoker and an expensive scotch drinker at the best chance he could, to be a smudge in the corner of the same picture as the folks that meant something in the society for their status and affluence, but certainly no amount of dress up could make Edmund Hall the kind of man that was able to say no to Fitzhugh White. Not in this lifetime.

He sat in the back of the steamcart as the men drove him all the away to the mines. Archie and another man that looked like he'd seen some things as the battlefront for either the mines or war, judging by the scarring that patterned one side of his face, had appeared at the house merely moments past dawn and told him Fitzhugh requested his presence. But it did not seem like a request at all, so he simply grabbed his coat and cane and followed the men, uninterested in finding out what could become of him if he said no.

He had not a single clue as to the whereabouts of the man that owned the house he'd slept in that night — if one could actually call sitting on the chair by an oil lamp in the main hall and listening for sounds of the door for Howard to appear, till he nodded off and woke in another minute, a sleep. The last he'd seen of his friend had really been two nights before, when Howard had left him for the study after dinner to go through the ledger he had obtained from Bryce Allen, the man he has since been accused of murdering.

Edmund could not fathom why anyone would make such accusations against Howard, even more, he did know how anyone would believe it. The Howard he knew was hardly the kind of man that wanted a confrontation, and albeit the man has the tendencies to be a tad obsessive when he was after something, Edmund could not imagine a situation where the auditor would take another man's life. Howard's father had a pistol, one he'd never actually seen the chap carry or use since he'd known him; it used to sit in a metal box in the lower drawer of the desk in the study, the box which was empty when Edmund checked in that evening after the royal guards had finally left the house. But he still could not think of a truth in the rumor.

Howard had left for the docks with a shipment from the mines on Fitzhugh's request the morning before, and against his better judgement, the auditor had decided he did not need him to come along. Now Howard had since not returned to the house, and he suddenly had become a fugitive too, wanted for the murder of a mam he had met with two days before in regard of Fitzhugh's affairs at the mines. Edmund's squeeze tightened in the fists he made as the steamcart halted in at the rocks, close the entrance of one of the caves.

They alighted the vehicle and Edmund turned in the direction of Fitzhugh's office, only to be slapped on the shoulder by the man with the terror of a scar on his face. Edmund halted in his track and faced them.

"Sir Fitzhugh's not at the office now, he's down in the caves. That's where you will be meeting him." Archie walked ahead of him and the other man in the direction of the hole in the rocks, with the other man standing his ground, waiting for the auditor's accomplice to lead.

Edmund Hall was born in the south, he played in the harshness of the colonies like every other kid his age back then, the landscape was raw and often unkempt in the areas the children often wondered to for a sense of adventure in the absence of fancy toys and proper gatherings, and one of those included rocks that had small caves that sometimes led into the ground where animals hid. The day he discovered he hated tight spaces was when his friends played a prank on him by dumping him in one of the holes and pulling a large branch over the opening, scurrying off in laughter. He'd screamed his lungs out till they came back and laughed at him even more, and he'd got off running after they helped him out, with his face reddened and swollen, and snort mixing with the tears running down his lean lips. He'd never as much as been near a hole since then. The room he slept in was perhaps the second largest in space after Howard's. More than often, he left the door to the private convenience open when he used the loo, Edward Hall was terrified of tight spaces, and Fitzhugh White was waiting for him inside a hole in a rock.

Fitzhugh stood by two oil lamps planted on sticks that were buried between rocks, he watched as a left-handed miner went to work with his pickaxe and chipped at the fresh face of the rock, hoping for something. Archie arrived by his side and not long after, Edmund appeared accompanied by the other man. They were a fair fifty yards inside the rock, with the peak of daylight lost after a few turns in the hole.

Fitzhugh tapped at the miner before he turned to see his guest, and the worker got up and left the scene, leaving his pickaxe behind, so that it was just Edward, himself and his men in the secrecy underneath the earth. "Edward, I'm glad you're here," he started.

Edward stood a couple of steps from the man, and swallowed the real response he wanted to give to Fitzhugh, wanting to be out of the cave already. "Of course, sir Fitzhugh, why wouldn't I?" he said.

"Shame, what the news is about your friend, Howard. He seems to have gotten himself in quite the pickle. You wouldn't happen to know his whereabouts, would you? For the royal guards' ears, of course."

"I'm afraid I do not s—sir, and if I must say, Master Forsyth is no murderer, I believe there's been a very big misunderstanding." Edward answered, trying his best to hide his growing discomfort.

"Well, I think that's left for the royal guards do decide. But the thing is, Edmund, I can help Howard. I can help make certain that the situation he's found himself in is resolved. But you see, Howard does not seem to care for my assistance. He practically told me off when I offered it yesterday even after he'd come spewing some delusions that's could make a stuffed bird laugh. I worry for that man even if he doesn't seem to know, Edmund, but he doesn't seem to worry for much, as he so claims."

"Master Howa—"

Fitzhugh did not let him speak, "I didn't ask you here to tell me of what he did or did not do, Edmund, if you're going to keep repeating yourself. Like I said, I want to help him, but I can't seem to know for the life of me what it is that will truly make him see reason. Perhaps you do?"

Edmund stayed silent as the sound of his heart thumping waywardly in his chest travelled throughout his entire body. It was difficult to tell which of the terrors was getting to him the most; the notorious former soldier who had him alone in a cave with his henchmen or the cave itself that seemed to be getting smaller with each passing moment.

"What is it that Howard Forsyth cares for more than making certain that things fall apart with my affairs here, Edmund?"

"He's a determined man, Master Howard, like a dog with a bone, and I'm afraid he has not shared with me

109

anything I can think of that falls in the category of what you so speak," Edmund finally spoke, his fists had returned to their form; one almost crushing his cane, and the other batting his side quite subtly as the anxiousness boiled still.

"Of course, you're a decent man yourself, aren't you? I would be disappointed if you had no sliver of loyalty in you. That is a quality for men with class and repute, truly. But you see, Edmund, Howard is not doing himself any favors stirring up a storm. I, have an army at my disposal, and can weather whatever comes my way. But he doesn't as it is apparent. Left to say you cannot do him any favors if he's captured by the authorities. And you, well, I suppose you have plans for when he goes down."

Edmund was resting almost his entire weight on his cane, if it were kicked away from him, the man would fall to the ground and perhaps crumble before anything else was done to him. Fitzhugh's words rang into his ears as he pondered quickly the things he was saying. The man had remained civil, but he was unsure if, and for how long he would continue to be. He did not know if he would survive whatever turn Fitzhugh took, as he just wanted to be out of that cave.

"I see you're thinking, Edmund, think well. There are a lot of things that can come of someone like me regarding you as valuable, a countless number of things, in affluence and proper regard alike. But need I tell you there are also as many things that can become of you if

I choose that that the air between us is not that which pleases me. Which will it be, Edmund?"

Hall was a hustler before and when he met Howard. He was still one. Howard though had accepted him in spite of his demeanors and for his prudent appearance. The man had not seen the things that he desired as a fool's chase by a pauper. Howard had acted like a friend to him even when he needn't be, he'd never been condescending as a plethora of even the middle-class folks he'd come across. Howard had trusted him with the affairs of his household at a time when no one would allow him near theirs. The man had trusted him his deepest secret. Edmund was a hustler that Howard found and believed in. So he let out a cough as his chest seemed to tighten, the panic reaching its bream. He gripped harder on his cane, turned and saw the scar-faced man still there, he looked at Archie and returned his gaze on Fitzhugh. "I have nothing to say to you," he said.

Adeline dressed in the fanciest dress she could find in her wardrobe, Saleh had even helped her to a bit of makeup, just enough to be proper but not so to make her glaring. The result was an incredibly stunning young woman. She had no proper shoes to fit her bell gown so she wore her work boots underneath, knowing that they would still be concealed. There was hardly enough time for madam Saleh to work her through the basics of female etiquettes by the women of the elite class, so Adeline was left to work with her wits.

A carriage was hailed as it was the most efficient and effective way to get her out without drawing the attention of onlookers as to why an elite was in the home of madam Saleh. Adeline used the umbrella which Howard had gotten her a while ago to hide her profile from people on the street until they were in the better parts of Greene County, where it was considered normal for people who were similarly dressed to be seen.

The coachman alighted from the horse-drawn carriage to help Adeline down. She thanked him before he left, drawing a look of surprise from the coachman before he left. She turned to face the Bryce building, the object of her quest. She watched two ladies walk by, trying to emulate their mannerisms. After a moment of staring, Adeline lifted her head, tilting it upwards a bit and walking purposefully in a strut that was ineffective as a conventional manner of walking, but fully enabled her to swing her hips in a subtle but provocative manner.

As she approached the door, she noticed a man in a long dark coat and a suit underneath. He wore a monocle that had a gold rim and a top hat that looked eerily familiar to Sir Dayton's. He smiled at Adeline as she turned her head at his call. She didn't know who he was and instantly became wary. He could be the murderer for all she knew, so she turned away as he walked towards her.

"Hello there! May I have a word with the lady?"

She tapped the door lightly, in a womanly manner as Saleh had told her, but she feared it wasn't loud enough and no one would hear. She wasn't wrong; the man with the monocle was soon encompassing her peripheral vision. She turned towards him slowly, with a forced smile spread across her face. He was a large man, something his coat did nothing to hide. Adeline wondered what line of business a man like him would do to attain such status.

"I am Rudolph John-Wesley, owner of the John-Wesley scotch brewery. I could not help but notice such a fine lady as yourself walk by."

"I'm very flattered Sir John-Wesley. Truly, I am…"

"Why then. Might I interest you in a drink? I would love to know all about you Lady…?"

Adeline panicked, clearing her throat loudly as she realized that they had not thought of a name. Her eyes darted left and right, trying to come up with a name. She saw the fur windbreaker strewn across his neck dangling in the early morning sun. John-Wesley shifted his weight to the other foot, subtle sign of discomfort and impatience. Adeline blurted out the first thing that came to mind.

"Adele… Fur skin. I am Adele Furskin. It is a pleasure to meet you, Sir John Wesley."

"Please, it's Rudolph. And, that name. I've never heard that. You're certainly not from around here."

"No. I'm from the west of the county and I'm in a bit of a hurry. If you don't mind, Sir John-Wesley?"

He scoffed. Men of his social standing were rarely ever rejected by women towards whom he made advances. Adeline's abrupt dismissal caught him on the back foot and sent him reeling. "Well I best not keep the lady. Perhaps some other time."

The door was answered a few moments later by the servant. His eyes looked tired and the stench of alcohol bathed him. He stared at Adeline for almost five seconds before waving her in. She was a little surprised that he had asked no questions about who she was or what she wanted, but she would take a victory where ever she found it. She followed him through the foyer and took a seat in the main entrance hall.

The servant walked around for a bit, before returning with a bottle of liquor in hand. He looked like he had seen better days and simply wished for everything that plagued him to be abolished, but he knew the universe was never that. He took a large swig of the drink, contorted his face wildly as it went down his throat. He let out a burp, unbothered with his guest.

"I was hoping…"

"You're the sister, yes?" He asked, obviously drunk. Something Adeline knew was always a good talking point.

"Yes."

"You've come to… for his body?"

"No, no not yet. I want to ask some questions regarding the incidents surrounding his death."

"He's dead. What incidents do you want to know?"

"Well. What I hear is that a man called Howard Forsyth killed him."

"Damn right! And don't let anyone tell you anything different."

"I believe you. But how did Howard kill him?"

"Why are you asking all these questions Ms. Allen. Just take the body… take the body and go." he stuttered.

"Well, I need to know what I would tell the coroner. I need these details to tell him. How did Bryce Allen die?"

"Forsyth killed him."

"Yes, Howard Forsyth. And how did he do it?"

"He... He did the thing, with… he put it in his food, like the man said."

"What thing?"

"It was poison." He blurted out, spittle dropping out the sides of his mouth. He cleaned it off with a sleeve and sniffed intensely.

"Yes, I know that. And who put it there? Who poisoned him?"

The silence was thick. He didn't need to speak for Adeline to know. The servant had poisoned Bryce and now was overwhelmed with guilt. But it didn't make sense to Adeline, why would the servant blame it on Howard? He would gain nothing from sending the auditor to jail, so why set him up? The servant began crying silently, his sobs now coming more and more.

"I was asked to do it. Men from the mines... they came and they paid me so well, but threatened me if I didn't do as they expected. I had no other... other choice. They said they would kill me."

"They won't hurt you. I promise you that, I will make sure the guards take who was responsible. No harm will come to you, I assure you. It..."

"I did it! The men... the men asked me to, but... I did it. I could have said no. I could have gone to the guards. But they would... no, the guards don't listen to men like me. I am a servant and nothing more. They won't be able to help me. So I did it Ms. Allen. I killed your brother, and when... I told them it was the Forsyth m...." his ramblings became incoherent as he began wailing uncomfortably.

Adeline sat still, feeling pity for him. In their society, the guards would never respond to the crisis of those of the lowest bracket. They were of little importance to anyone. All disputes that required the external intervention of the law to quench any altercations of the lower class was waved aside, considered as a squirmish of animals. She let the servant express his pent-up emotions as she waited quietly, after a moment, he tried to regain control of himself, slowing his sniffling and body spasms as much as he could.

"I'm sorry you… you had to see that." He said, trying to clear his head of the effects of the alcohol.

"It's alright. We need to tell this to the guards, otherwise this Forsyth man could be in some serious trouble. And I know the last thing you want to do, is to have another death on your hands."

"No. Never. I will pay for this great injustice I have done."

"I'm truly sorry you were coerced into doing this. I will have a word with Lord Palmerston, perhaps he will find a way to make your sentence lighter. But in the meantime, you have to make this confession you've given me to him. Can you do that?"

"I don't know if I can."

"Yes, you can. If there is going to be justice, this is what you must do."

Adeline gave comforting words to the servant, reassuring him of the days to come. He was young, and scared to the bone. But after a while, Adeline was confident that he would speak to Palmerston and help clear Howard. He promised her that he would remain out of sight till he saw that Palmerston had come to town. She left the house later in the afternoon, walking out to the street. She propped open her umbrella and began walking home, keeping a lookout for a carriage.

She changed her mind about returning to the slums dressed the way she was, and took a detour to the Forsyth home. She entered through the rear entrance that was hidden away from the main street as two coppers hung out in front, doing their best to look casual but failing badly. She quickly changed out of the gown into a blouse with a laced fitting behind and a skirt. She let her hair down her shoulders and wiped most of the makeup from her face.

She left the way she'd come, feeling comfortable now as she once again became a shadow in the streets. No one in that part of town noticed people like her. They were there for errands and weren't considered in the least bit vital to the growth of society, but yet, they were its backbone. The smell of fried fish nearby drew her attention. The fish reminded her of the sea and the sea of Lord Palmerston. He would be on his way to Greene County and everything would turn out alright.

Someone waved a hand at her from her far left, causing her to turn her head, looking. It was John-Wesley, smiling at her. She paused for a moment, confused as to how he was still able to recognize her after she had a change of clothes. Adrenaline rushed through her bloodstream as her brain made the connection, she was being followed. As she took a step to run, she felt a large forearm go across her neck and a piece of cloth soaked in some odorless liquid went across her nostrils, knocking her unconscious.

EIGHT

"I can't wait anymore. There is barely two hours of sunlight left. We need to find Adeline."

"Just let Chevonne return. She knows the town well, if anyone saw something, Chevonne will find out. Adeline will be back soon; she is probably just caught up in something. Perhaps she was summoned by the Dayton household again." Saleh spoke from her place in the chair, staring warily at the door.

She knew Adeline just as well as she knew herself. Something had gone wrong and Adeline was gone. Howard felt it too, but it was illogical to let him run out to go find her. Saleh couldn't stop him if he made up his mind to go after her, but she would do what she could. If something truly had come up, Adeline would send word through someone on the streets and it would get to Saleh soon enough. But with the hours counting by, there was nothing.

Howard looked even more tense; Saleh could see the vein which had popped out on the side of his head pulsing. He felt it too, something was off and he was fighting the compelling desire to go after her. Howard looked through the peeking slot in the door, eyes scanning the streets outside for any sign of Adeline or the Irish girl who had answered the door when he first arrived. It was buzzing with people, all of them, similarly dressed making it hard for Howard to keep track.

He watched as men and women and children walked to and fro, going about their businesses. Children, some as young as five, Hawked wares of baked bread and boiled corn around for people to buy. Farmers too hauled their produce over their shoulders, pulling it to their homes for storage. Their kids followed close behind, covered in dirt and grime. Howard couldn't understand why the financial divide was so. If only the Queen had let her resources reach places like these, perhaps life there would be better.

Howard imagined a world where everyone was equal and no one had to struggle for much. As a child, his father made him earn every gift by performing a task, either academic or house duties. Even for every meal he ate, he had worked for it, but not in a manner that would be considered inhumane, just in the right proportions. Whatever the outcome of the following hours, Howard swore to take the issues he had seen to Lord Palmerston and the Queen and perhaps try to change things.

"Someone took her." Chevonne announced as she walked in through the back entrance. "Two men, one was a well-dressed man who no one could recognize, but the other, they say the bloke works for Fitzhugh."

"I have to go."

"Howard if you leave now, you will be walking right into a trap." Saleh spoke, the words rushing out of her mouth as fear began to take hold.

Howard wasn't listening. He found a bunch of papers that he had been scribbling into and gathered them into a satchel. If Fitzhugh had gone after her, then he had no choice. He would make a deal with him, one that would determine the fate of Adeline. Saleh stood by the door, blocking his path. But she connected with his eyes, seeing the conviction in them and knowing that there was no stopping him.

"Just bring her home." Salah spoke as she stepped out of his way.

Howard ran out the house into the streets. He needed to get to the mines and the fastest way was through the main market was on a horse. Saleh had only one horse, one he couldn't take and while he did have three back at his house, he couldn't risk going there. He considered stealing a horse, another crime that was taken seriously by law, thanks to the Queen, but he was running out of options.

He walked through the market briskly, after spotting a man who had just gotten off his horse. He didn't seem to pay much attention to the animal, and more intent on speaking to the local townsfolk. Howard made a quick dash for it, but right before he made contact, its rider turned around, spotting him. A look of recognition across his face right before he screamed so loud, it shocked Howard.

"He's right here! Get him!"

Howard turned and ran, noticing a group of men trying to squeeze their way through the market crowd to get him. They were armed, but didn't pull their weapons on him, giving Howard the notion that they were guards and not Fitzhugh's men. He ran through market stalls, tripping up the wares of the people who sold them, instinctively shouting out apologies as he ran.

The men gave chase, trying their best not to lose him in the crowd. They watched for where the commotion was and ran in that direction, hoping to catch him. Howard took a left turn and jumped over a table before tripping over a sack of potatoes. He rolled to the side of the path which was filled with people, fitting his body right by the base of a stall. The young girl who sold the potatoes watched the entire scene unfold before she smiled and raised her index finger to her lips.

"He went that way! Behind the fruit stand! Hurry!"

The men didn't even bother to check for who was shouting off instructions. They appreciated it nonetheless and took off running for the fruit stand. Howard thanked the girl before turning back in the direction he had come. As expected, the horse was left there unguarded as Howard mounted the animal and set off to the mines. The sun had begun its final descent behind him as he whipped the horse with the reins, urging it to go faster, the only thought on his mind was the lady he had dragged into the debacle.

As he arrived at the mine, he noticed something odd. It was entirely devoid of life. He knew that there were always a few people left behind to look over things before the next work day, and they would be found around the mines around fires or just seen walking the length of the ridges and cliffs along the mines, but there was no one in sight. A few torches lit up the walls outside, between them was a cave, with the ambient orange hue of another open flame coming from within.

Howard jumped off the horse, pulling out the pistol he had. Taking the guard's horse paid off with a few extra bullets and a fistful of gunpowder in the horse's saddle. He didn't bother sneaking in as he knew they would be waiting for him, so he went in, holding the pistol outstretched in his hand. The cave was a lot higher than the others he had been in, its passage was slightly curved, making it difficult to see more than a few meters ahead without obstruction of the rock walls.

The lights coming from the end of the cave became brighter and warmer, indicating that he was nearing his target. He let his finger slide around the outer guard and rest on the trigger. He hoped greatly he would not have to use the gun, but If it came to it, Howard told himself that he would shoot Fitzhugh in the head and try to take out as many others as he could before he would be taken down, giving Adeline a chance to escape. His gut told him how illogical his intent was; he had barely healed from his experience on the train the previous day, one he'd only been simply lucky to survive, but his heart had taken the lead and would not listen.

"Howard, you finally get to join us."

It took all of his willpower not to pull the trigger instantly at the voice as his brain interpreted the scene before him. Men that totaled about eight in number, all armed wandering in a semicircle, facing Howard. Fitzhugh was the only one seated on what looked like a stump in the middle of the clearing inside the cave that was lined seemingly endlessly with torches. His relaxed demeanor still emanating from his very being. To his left stood Archie, the man who had, on multiple occasions, driven Howard to the mines. Howard saw one of the men holding Adeline by her hair. A piece of cloth tied around her mouth and a blade to her neck. His face looked as though he was begging for the order to be given. Howard pointed the gun straight at him, resulting in the other men pointing theirs back at the auditor.

"You arrive and the first thing you do is put a gun in my face? Not ver—"

"Drop the horsecrap, Fitzhugh. This has nothing to do with her. Let her go, let's settle this." He slowly put his hand into the satchel he wore across his neck and produced the ledger. "I have here with me, all the evidence I need to make certain of your conviction for all the atrocities you've dallied in at this mine. I will let you have it, just let her go."

"You're asking me to send off my only means of bargain? Now why would I do that?"

"Because I'm giving you what you want. Now, here! Take it!" He flung the ledger across the rocky floor towards them, returning his arm to the pistol. "Take it and you'll never see me or her again."

"Howard, look. I appreciate the gesture, I really do. But you don't really understand me. I need a man like you with me with what I have planned. This war, the one started by Queen Victoria. It doesn't hurt her, not as much as it does you and I. We have all lost someone in this war, been affected by it in some way. But I wouldn't be one to just let it go like that. Which is why I will take back whatever I can from this war. No one is innocent, so I'll be taking from both sides."

Adeline struggled, making muffling sounds as the man pulled harder on her hair. Howard had to open his mouth slightly to control his breathing. One accident and it would all be over. Fitzhugh noticed he had caught Howard between a rock and a hard place, the thought filled him with confidence. He continued.

"I'm sure you've wondered where all the money and materials have been going to? Well, I'll tell you. Imagine an army of men, all equipped with state-of-the-art machinery powered by our steam engines and gear technology. Steamcarts would revolutionize war! Troops would be deployed faster and further than ever before! All of that, could be available to either side of the war… for the highest bidder."

"You want to betray your country, for money?" Howard spat.

"The country betrayed me first. It's only fair that they get what has been coming all this time. Howard, I need you in this new world which I'm trying to build. A man like you would be a worthy ally, a powerful one too. By the time we're done, we would have enough wealth to do whatever we wanted. More than the peanuts Palmerston has offered you. Imagine what that would mean for this lady of yours here, to become a first-class citizen. And all you have to do, is join me."

Howard forehead pulled as a million possibilities ran through his mind, the air in the cave became heavier with the tension, making it hard for him to breathe, "Let her go first."

"No. See our mutual friend did say that she would be the one thing that would make you do whatever it is I want. And what I want is for you to join me." Fitzhugh nodded at the man with the knife who in turn smiled with a confirming nod, a maniacal grin across his face as he poised to run the blade through her.

"What do you say, Forsyth? It would be a shame to have to kill the two of you."

He had lost. If he refused, Adeline would die and he would as well, considering that he was well outnumbered. His mind gave him only one order—ensure the safety of Adeline. He kept his pistol trained on the man with the knife to her throat, before turning his eyes to Fitzhugh. The captain of the mines looked relaxed as ever, not even breaking into a sweat in the humidity of the cave. It was obvious, Howard gave his response.

"Alr..."

"Howard Forsyth! By the order of her majesty the Queen, I place you under a..."

Everyone turned to see the royal guards all crammed into the front entrance of the cave, right behind Howard. They looked shocked at the sight of a man holding a knife to a lady's throat. Howard seized the distraction as his chance and fired. The bullet hit the man in the left shoulder, causing him to drop the knife from the force of the projectile. He stumbled backwards, letting go of her hair.

The bullets began flying as the guards opened fire on the miners believing they had fired the preemptive shot. Adeline and Howard went flat against the floor, crawling as quickly as they could towards each other. Fitzhugh disappeared behind a bunch of rocks as the bullets began to come more frequently. The guards had come in their numbers with the hopes of catching Howard by circling and outnumbering him. They had followed him after he took the horse and waited for the right moment to pounce, their timing could not have been better for him.

They hid behind boulders, exchanging shots with Fitzhugh's men trying to take down whoever they could. Soon the cave was filled with the acrid stench of gunpowder and smoke. The guards had the upper hand, with a larger amount of the ammunition, they could remain engaged in the exchange longer than the miners, so they dug in, firing back. But what came next, they weren't prepared for it.

Fitzhugh broke out from the floor underneath them in the machine he had used to help the collapsed miners escape. It looked like it had been updated and retrofitted for more agility as there appeared to be more gears and crankshafts running underneath its chassis. The steam engine huffed and blew hot air out at intervals from the back of the contraption. Even the center piece that held Fitzhugh had been updated with a hard metal shell to protect him.

The guards fired at the machine, but copper bullets did nothing but bounce off the steel frame of the machine. It brought down a large metal fist on a guard, clamping onto his body with its vice-like grip, before throwing him into the rocks that hit the rest of the guards. The shooting continued as the guards retreated. Howard and Adeline followed suit, rushing for the exit as well. Fitzhugh smacked a fist into a boulder, pulling it straight from the floor and shoved it right into them.

Howard pushed Adeline forwards as the large rock struck the roof of the cave, shattered and struck him on the shoulder. She got back to her feet and helped him up as they continued running for the exit. Two guards had made it outside waiting with their guns aimed at the one way in and out of the cave. Howard and Adeline rushed out, throwing their hands in the air the sign of the pointed guns. The attention of the officers quickly went from them to the large man-driven machine behind them

Fitzhugh threw another boulder at the guard on his left who had begun firing at him. It smashed against his head, crushing the man instantly. His colleague dropped his weapon and ran, fear getting the best of him. Howard put Adeline behind him. There was no way he would be able to do anything that could stop a machine like that, as the powerful rifles of the guard couldn't dent it, his pistol would be of no effect. He pulled out the weapon and began firing at him, finishing all six bullets in the gun in seconds.

Fitzhugh used the vice to grab Howard, lifting him effortlessly clear off the floor before smashing him back into it. His shoulder blades connected with the hard-stone floor. The pain fired through every receptor in his body, nearly causing him to black out. Adeline screamed.

"You've ruined everything! All you had to do was agree to become richer than everyone you'd ever known! What is wrong with you?"

He lifted Howard off the floor again, and flung him into a rock near the edge of a cliff. He heard a sharp crack as his midsection bounced off the rock. He dropped to the floor as the taste of blood began to fill his mouth. He tried to prop himself up to his knees, but his body buckled under the intense pain. Fitzhugh rushed at him, picking up the auditor again and smacking him again on the floor. Adeline couldn't stand to watch anymore, so she picked up the rifle the guard had thrown and fired at Fitzhugh.

He turned with a flick of his mechanized arm and knocked Adeline backward against the edge of the cliff. Through the stabbing pain and blurred vision of near death, Howard watched as Adeline staggered off the cliff, but with the last of her strength managed to hold onto the edge with both hands. Howard crawled on his stomach to the edge of the cliff and grabbed her hands. With Howard's help, she managed to shimmy up and she remained unconscious next to Howard.

"This is all your fault, Forsyth!" Fitzhugh bent over and picked Howard up again, this time aiming to finish him off. The auditor didn't fight back, having nothing left physically to offer. He closed his eyes and waited for the final killing blow. A shot rang out in the darkness and struck metal. When Howard opened his tired eyes, he could see over Fitzhugh's shoulder to the shooter: Archie.

Fitzhugh quickly rebounded, dropping Howard, who hit the ground. You would think the bullet would have actually hit Fitzhugh, but that was not the case. Archie had aimed his shot perfectly and fired a projectile into the gearbox of the machine. The projectile had severed the hydraulics of the machine that held the large unit upright. Without the hydraulics to hold it up, it would be dependent only on its carrier. But that was physically impossible, because the whole thing weighed almost a ton. There was a loud cracking sound as the entire weight of the machine fell off Fitzhugh and his femur cracked from the pressure.

Howard watched the scene unfold before him as shock and confusion led to disbelief and pain. He closed his eyes and let the darkness engulf him.

NINE

S he had been pregnant only once in her life, forty years ago by a man she thought loved her beyond measure. They had not been very public with their affections. But if she had thought that the news that she was carrying a child for him would have made him change his mind, she might have told him, and maybe he would have stayed. But maybe she would have lost him anyway, because his eyes had suddenly found the daughter of a consultant. And if she hadn't lost her child, Saleh might have had something to remind her of the best time of her life as a young woman. So, she had spent it imagining a life with Nicholas Forsyth.

But she had found herself a child in the misfit girl who knocked on her door nearly two decades later. The moment Adeline had entered her home, the woman had felt a new will to live unlike anything she had experienced in a long time. It had been sick, perhaps, to be glad that the child had no ward. But she had been glad that fate had brought her someone to soothe her heart, even if she had not been open about it at first.

Adeline was only a young girl, and yet Saleh had seen a fire in her eyes like she had once had in her own when she had been about the girl's age. The girl was quick on her feet and rarely left anyone alone who thought they could take advantage of her. She quickly understood the things she was shown and needed little help to do even the bigger things. The child could have taken on even the queen and perhaps the whole world if she had been allowed. Adeline had come to her as a laden but broken vessel.

The day she discovered this was the very first night the girl spent under her roof. Saleh granted her a bed in the only room that was not yet occupied, out of the four in her house. She was to spend the night sharing the bed with another girl who was a little older than her and also worked as a helper. Saleh had wandered into the girls' room in the middle of the night and found Adeline curled up on the bare floor, mumbling silently to herself in her sleep. She had watched her do this for nearly an hour before finally waking the girl and getting her to lie back down on the bed. The following night, Saleh had found her doing the same thing, and it had worried the woman. On the third night of her stay in their house, Saleh had let Adeline sleep with her on the bed in her own room, and the girl had snuggled up to her and slept like a baby.

If it had been up to her, she would never have allowed Adeline to seek the help of another person. But Adeline wasn't going to be fobbed off with the talk, and said she wanted to take care of herself. And so, when Edmund Hall had come to her that day and asked for a girl to help the Forsyth household, she had thought of all she had gone through and hoped that Adeline would have a better chance with a man who bore that name.

She might have lost his child and be heartbroken that she was not the one he chose, but Nicholas was a man she had never stopped loving, and the things she had said to his son the night before when Howard sought refuge with her were a game to take the words out of his mouth.

She knew very well who he was. Adeline had begun to change not months after she started working for him, and soon the girl had betrayed her affection for the man. Saleh had been afraid for her at first, because she had heard about other girls from the south. She knew they had thought the same of themselves and their high-ranking masters, only to be ruined or worse hanged if they were ever caught. But Adeline would be wiser than she, and in her fear, Saleh was glad for the happiness the girl had found, even if she could never share it.

She had heard nothing since Adeline had walked out the door that morning. Saleh had been supportive when she'd said she'd look for Bryce's killer last night, but she couldn't shake the fear. She hadn't felt like eating the breakfast Chevonne had made. She had skipped lunch, too, because she was focused on Adeline walking back through the doors she sat staring at.

Every moment had passed, and it was as if her heart was growing darker and darker, she could almost feel that the girl had been in trouble before the news of her abduction reached her, and then Howard had gone after her, and now he had been gone almost as long.

Chevonne hadn't bothered to eat from the dinner she had prepared herself. She had settled down next to the old lady, who had become very quiet in the last few hours while they kept hopeful watch. There was no need to tell her what the woman felt, Adeline was not her biological child, but Madam Saleh took her as such.

Saleh was almost on her feet before Chevonne when they heard the sound of the carriage trotting in front of the house, and they were both at the door before a knock was heard.

Relieved and startled, they saw Howard and Adeline enter leaning on each other. Adeline was supporting his battered body more than he was supporting hers.

"How did this happen?" asked Saleh.

While Chevonne tended them both and nursed their wounds, they told Saleh the whole story. With a last effort, they both finally dragged themselves to beds Saleh had made ready for them.

EPILOGUE

"Howard?" The voice sounded distant, his body felt lifeless, his eyes were blurry. "Howard? Can you hear me?"

He blinked slowly, one moment at a time, until his vision was clear enough and he could make out the image of the person speaking. The man's white hair grew full around his beard, and his eyes peered through the hollows under his brows. Lord Palmerston had always been a handsome sight, even before the gray had taken over his face. Howard's brows lifted and he nodded. He wanted to get up, but moving a muscle that wasn't in his face felt like a task that would kill him.

"Please, stay in your bed. The doctor says you have suffered many injuries, many of which will take time to heal, he says you are really lucky to be alive. Adeline, thankfully, is doing quite a bit better, but she too is still in bed recovering."

Howard tried to speak, but his lips felt so weak.

"Save your strength, please. The doctor gave you something for the pain, it may keep you in bed for a long time, but you can hear me. Let me do the talking.

It would be an understatement to say that what you both did took a tremendous amount of courage; you have no idea how many people went up against Fitzhugh and did not survive to tell their story. Consider that my tribute and a sign of my respect.

I have had suspicions about Fitzhugh and the mines for almost three years, but I have never been able to find a way to prove them. I received your letter. I was surprised to find your letter of invitation via Sir Archibald Dayton, but then Archie sent a message as well, and I knew I had to be here no matter what."

Howard's eyes widened at the mention of Fitzhugh's right hand.

"Oh yes, I suppose I should apologize for keeping you in the dark about Archie, he's been my eyes and ears regarding Fitzhugh for a little over a year, but there was pretty little he could do without risking Fitzhugh finding out. His news of you and Fitzhugh came only a few hours before Sir Dayton's letter, and I made arrangements to be here at once."

"I want you to know that the extent of your efforts is greatly appreciated. Her Majesty the Queen herself will honor you both as soon as you have recovered your strength. For your friend, Her Majesty has even provided an elevation to your rank. A most extraordinary gesture."

"You should also know that the real killer of Bryce Allen has confessed. He could no longer live with the guilt. He has mentioned you both, and your words and

Adeline's will carry great weight at the trial." Lord Palmerston spoke like a man who knew that the kingdom probably owed its continued existence to the two of them.

Lord Palmerston rose from the chair beside his bed, ready to take his leave, "I should let you rest more now. I'll be back to check on you soon. Thank you, Howard," the man said as he walked to the door, leaving the auditor alone in the room.

"My dear mother, may she rest in peace, used to say that the evil of which a man's heart is capable is infinite, just like the good. Fitzhugh White was a man I knew for his evil; Archie Gilbert I came to know as the good he really was. And it seems my closest ally has betrayed me."

"I knew Edmund Hall was a hustler from the first day I met him, but I trusted that he would become something more. It seems I was wrong, very wrong. I haven't bothered to ask Archie what happened to him. I can't bring myself to think of ever seeing his face again, for I might become capable of murder after all."

"Adeline and I can now marry. With her extraordinary elevation to my rank by the Queen, nothing now stands in the way of our personal happiness. Her Majesty has learned that a southern girl, whom she so detests, has saved her mine and ensured that her enemies can no longer be armed. For a very long time we discussed whether we could accept such an elevation while nothing changed in society. For the sake of our

love, we finally agreed and because we believe this is the only way we can continue to make a difference. We dream of changing the order of things so that class does not determine how people live and who they love. Together, we will continue to work for that justice."

www.ingramcontent.com/pod-product-compliance
Lightning Source LLC
Chambersburg PA
CBHW050454110726
47899CB00003B/931